## PRAISE FOR M. L. BUCHMAN

Tom Clancy fans open to a strong female lead will clamor for more.

— *Drone*, Publishers Weekly

Superb! Miranda is utterly compelling!

— *Booklist,* starred review

Miranda Chase continues to astound and charm.

— Barb M.

Escape Rating: A. Five Stars! OMG just start with *Drone* and be prepared for a fantastic binge-read!

— Reading Reality

The best military thriller I've read in a very long time. Love the female characters.

— *Drone,* Sheldon McArthur, founder of The Mystery Bookstore, LA

A fabulous soaring thriller.

Meticulously researched, hard-hitting, and suspenseful.

Expert technical details abound, as do realistic military missions with superb imagery that will have readers feeling as if they are right there in the midst and on the edges of their seats.

Buchman has catapulted his way to the top tier of my favorite authors.

Nonstop action that will keep readers on the edge of their seats.

M L. Buchman's ability to keep the reader right in the middle of the action is amazing.

— Long and Short Reviews

The only thing you'll ask yourself is, "When does the next one come out?"

— *Wait Until Midnight,* RT Reviews, 4 stars

The first...of (a) stellar, long-running (military) romantic suspense series.

— *The Night is Mine,* Booklist, "The 20 Best Romantic Suspense Novels: Modern Masterpieces"

I knew the books would be good, but I didn't realize how good.

— Night Stalkers series, Kirkus Reviews

Buchman mixes adrenalin-spiking battles and brusque military jargon with a sensitive approach.

— Publishers Weekly

13 times "Top Pick of the Month"

— Night Owl Reviews

# HEART OF A RUSSIAN BEAR DOG

## A WHITE HOUSE PROTECTION FORCE ROMANCE STORY

### M. L. BUCHMAN

Buchman Bookworks

# SIGN UP FOR M. L. BUCHMAN'S NEWSLETTER TODAY

*and receive:*
*Release News*
*Free Short Stories*
*a Free Book*

*Get your free book today. Do it now.*
*free-book.mlbuchman.com*

## Other works by M. L. Buchman: *(* - also in audio)*

## Other works by M. L. Buchman:

### Contemporary Romance (cont)

**Love Abroad**
*Heart of the Cotswolds: England*
*Path of Love: Cinque Terre, Italy*

**Where Dreams**
*Where Dreams are Born*
*Where Dreams Reside*
*Where Dreams Are of Christmas\**
*Where Dreams Unfold*
*Where Dreams Are Written*

### Science Fiction / Fantasy

**Deities Anonymous**
*Cookbook from Hell: Reheated*
*Saviors 101*

**Single Titles**
*The Nara Reaction*
*Monk's Maze*
*the Me and Elsie Chronicles*

### Non-Fiction

**Strategies for Success**
*Managing Your Inner Artist/Writer*
*Estate Planning for Authors\**
*Character Voice*
*Narrate and Record Your Own*
*Audiobook\**

## Short Story Series by M. L. Buchman:

### Romantic Suspense

**Delta Force**
*Th Delta Force Shooters*
*The Delta Force Warriors*

**Firehawks**
*The Firehawks Lookouts*
*The Firehawks Hotshots*
*The Firebirds*

**The Night Stalkers**
*The Night Stalkers 5D Stories*
*The Night Stalkers 5E Stories*
*The Night Stalkers CSAR*
*The Night Stalkers Wedding Stories*

**US Coast Guard**

**White House Protection Force**

### Contemporary Romance

**Eagle Cove**

**Henderson's Ranch\***

**Where Dreams**

### Action-Adventure Thrillers

**Dead Chef**

**Miranda Chase Origin Stories**

### Science Fiction / Fantasy

**Deities Anonymous**

**Other**
*The Future Night Stalkers*
*Single Titles*

# ABOUT THIS BOOK

*Alex Warren* and his Russian bear dog *Valentin* arrive in Washington, DC to join the Secret Service Uniformed Division. A boss who hates him on sight rapidly becomes the least of his problems.

*Tanya Larina,* Assistant Foreign Minister for Ukraine, has dedicated her life to maneuvering the Russians back out of Crimea. She has come to DC to sign a treaty with the American President as the first step in a long campaign.

When Alex pulls protection detail for Tanya, it's Valentin the bear dog who falls tail over paws in love with her on first sight. Can he convince Alex to follow his lead?

# 1

---

"DON'T YOU MIND THEIR SNEERS FOR ONE SINGLE SECOND," Alex Warren used his squeakiest high voice to cheer up his dog. The chill fog of his breath blanketed Valentin's furry face for a moment.

Valentin wagged his long tail slowly in agreement. Actually, being a dog, he would just be happy at the attention.

Not a chance that his massive Caucasian shepherd cared about the group of US Secret Service handlers and their Malinois and German shepherds waiting for their turn. Valentin wasn't the sort of dog to judge himself by others. Alex wished he could say the same for himself.

The Secret Service K-9 test-and-training course at the James J. Rowley Training Center was the most impressive one he'd ever seen. Behind them was the main building which included classrooms, kennels, and interiors for room-clearing and explosives-detection practice. Out here in the bitter February cold of a rural Maryland sunrise, the exterior course spread out over an acre of ground. There were agility courses, obedience and communication tests, and, of course, attack-and-takedown training.

And this was only the smallest corner of JJRTC where all DC Secret Service agents trained. This morning he'd come in past driving courses, an urban combat zone, and even a chunk of airliner fuselage and an old Marine One helo. He couldn't wait to try those.

No, Valentin wasn't threatened by the other dogs at all. It was easy to understand why, as even the largest was barely half Valentin's size.

But the other USSS handlers were bugging the crap out of Alex.

"Your Valentine looks like a rug, not a dog," Lieutenant Carlton, never Carl, Tibbets called out. Alex had learned that rule about the Lieutenant in his first two minutes after joining the Washington, DC, team this morning. San Francisco suddenly felt very far away.

"Val-en-*teen*. He's Russian, not a greeting card," Alex tried to stare the man down. But as they were both wearing sunglasses against the low, early-morning sun, it didn't seem to work very well.

"Valen*teen*. Yeah, right." Carlton clearly hadn't gotten his crème-filled donuts this morning. Instead he'd eaten a dose of nasty. Alex wondered if the guy had merely turned into an asshole or if he'd been born that way.

Alex patted Valentin's big head. He didn't have to reach down at all; the dog's head was waist high.

"Valen*teen!* Ooo! Ooo!" Bethany Wilson called out in

an overly prissy tone—one that still had her West Virginia twang behind it. "Y'all are going to have to say Valen*teen's* Day next week or there's gonna be a mess o' trouble." It earned her a laugh from most of the other guys. She was cute, funny, and a damn fine dog handler. She and her dog had been out to his old posting in San Francisco for a couple weeks last year. They never got together, but he'd certainly enjoyed her company. Her and her dog's demonstrations of just how "next level" DC was in the Secret Service dog world had played a major role in his transferring here.

Alex joined in the laugh easily. "Well, he *was* born on Valentine's Day. So making it Valentin's Day definitely works for him."

"Slow, big-assed piece of dogmeat who'll never keep up with my Malinois. Can't believe they let you two into the Secret Service at all." Carlton was just looking for a fight, but Alex didn't see any reason to give it to him.

But he didn't like it when someone insulted his sweet dog. He chose an underhanded jibe rather than a frontal assault.

"You're not like those hyperactive little Malinois fluffballs, are you?" Alex squeaked it to Valentin loud enough to earn a happy smile from his dog and some laughs down the line.

Except from Carlton Tibbets—probably *Junior,* or *the Third,* or *the Junior Third*—who turned to face him, and snapped out "Asshole!" in a nasty tone.

Before Alex could even think about reacting, Valentin spun on Carlton.

His deep snarl silenced the entire line.

The dog out on the course twisted to see what was happening, ran into a slalom pole, and tumbled to the ground.

Carlton's seventy-pound Malinois, Ripper, was the only one to step forward, bristling all the way down to his tail, ready for the command *Fass*—Attack!

Carlton, however, stumbled back and fell on his ass. Too bad the February cold snap had briefly frozen the muddy field grass.

No one else moved an inch.

Valentin wasn't called a Russian bear dog just because of his big square head. He and Alex weighed in at the same one-eighty—right at the top of his breed. His dog's long, shaggy coat was a pure dark brown, that was rare, except for a light tan chest blaze. He looked like a not-so-small shaggy bear and sounded like a royally pissed grizzly.

Alex called out the Russian command for Quiet, "*Tiho*." Then followed it with a soft "*Molodets*" for Good Boy.

Valentin silenced immediately but didn't look away from Carlton for an instant—he ignored the still-bristling Malinois as if Ripper was a three-pound Pomeranian, which somehow seemed to piss of Ripper even more.

Alex's was the only dog he knew of in the whole US Secret Service that was trained in Russian. German and occasionally English was a Service dog's normal command set.

When he'd been paired with Valentin two years ago, he'd tried to point out to his parents that his degree in the

Golden Age of Russian literature hadn't been *completely* wasted. They hadn't bought it. Up against their expectation of his joining the family's law firm that dated back to the days of the California Gold Rush, he supposed they never would.

Alex turned his back on Carlton, instead watching the German shepherd out on the course restart his run. After one low woof, that sounded more like a scoff of dismissal than a threat, Valentin did the same.

JJRTC's maples and oaks were still bare branch, so he could just hear the squealing tires from the defensive driving course a quarter mile to the west. The chill morning breeze carried just a hint of burning rubber as the Secret Service drivers skidded and spun their vehicles. Thankfully, the urban street for assault simulations that lay between them hadn't kicked into gear yet, so he could also hear the early morning birdsong.

"Hell of a first day," Lieutenant "Jerk" Jurgen, the head of the dog center at JJRTC, sneered as he walked up. Alex had only been in DC forty-eight hours and on duty for only these last two, but already knew the nickname was deserved. "Where's his goddamn leash?"

"I don't use one. We might weigh the same but a lot more of him is muscle than me, so the leash doesn't do much. He obeys my voice commands."

Jurgen grimaced at him. But he did think to let Valentin sniff him before offering a pat—always a smart move with a Caucasian shepherd as the breed wasn't noted for its friendliness to strangers. In fact, it was a dog to be approached carefully by anyone not identified as immediate family by its alpha handler. One of the many reasons they made such good guard dogs.

Jurgen gave Valentin time to make his own decision, and accept the gesture.

*The head trainer might be a jerk,* Bethany had told him when he'd called for some coming-East and first-day advice, *but he's a very skilled jerk who loves his dogs far more than his people.*

Alex was good with that.

Jurgen even squatted in front of Valentin and whispered to the dog.

Alex had to lean in to overhear.

"You *would* take on the lead ERT dog team on your first day. Good job!" He scrubbed his knuckles on the dog's head before moving on.

Alex glanced sideways at Carlton. The top Emergency Response Team? *Shit!* "Lead dog" might not be an official title, but no question DC was thick with hierarchy. If Carlton Tibbets and Ripper—as if someone named Carlton could possibly handle a dog named Ripper— were at the top, then it was more like Alex's first day in hell. Carlton was going to heap all the garbage he could manage on him and Valentin as payback.

The sun was a handspan above the horizon, but the temperature hadn't cracked twenty degrees yet—a bitter rarity Bethany had assured him. A couple of the short-coated Dobermans looked plaintively at their Secret Service handlers as they puffed out steamy breaths.

Valentin, however, was truly in his element. His shaggy coat was made for sleeping in snowstorms during a Russian winter. DC summers would be the challenge for him, in ways that a foggy and cold San Francisco summer could never be.

But when the Secret Service had said there was an opening on the DC team, the two of them had hit the ground running. Actually, they'd had a great week-long drive across the country in Alex's Jeep Wrangler, but same idea.

He dug his fingers deep into Valentin's soft undercoat to reassure himself and Valentin leaned against his thigh in response. They'd been the top of the dog heap in San Francisco. A much more informal world out there. Here they were the unknown, the outsiders. Chances were that after this morning's introduction, he'd be bottom-rostered until the day he retired.

Because hell, it *was* Washington, DC—the gold medal posting of the Secret Service. They'd done their "foreign" office time in the City by the Bay, and it was time to prove themselves. *That* he had no fear about.

He might miss the California girls, but maybe not that much. The chill fogs of his family's Nob Hill home and UC Berkeley were a far cry from Malibu bikini-land.

If Alex could just not have to deal with Carlton Tibbets on his first day.

Bethany ran her dog, a big German shepherd named Trixie of all silliness, into the course. Because, of course, you'd give a girl dog with a cutesy name to a pretty blonde. Jerk Jurgen had come by his nickname honestly —seemed to revel in it.

Not that Bethany or Trixie appeared to care; they did a fine job of working the course. A combination of voice and hand signals, they were well on their way to one of the top scores of the day.

Slalom through a line of spaced stakes to prove high-speed agility. Dive down into a twisting ten-yard by eighteen-inch tube at a full run. Exit at a full sprint, up a narrow walkway and across a six-inch wide bridge high over a water pool, and down a ladder on the far side. Clear a four-foot wall. Jump into a full-size pickup truck's window and put a bite on the "terrorist" driver mannequin. Then over a six-foot wall and take down a live runner in a thick, heavily padded bite suit.

That was just the first lap of the course.

Later, more agility work.

More bite work.

It was all part of weekly retraining and periodic testing to make sure that all of the dogs were kept up to standards.

It was also Valentin's first chance to prove that he qualified.

Today's group was all attack dogs.

There was some overlap. ERT dogs could find the most obvious explosives. And the sniffer dogs could attack—if they had to. Every dog here today, except Valentin, was a "pointy-ear"—breeds with sharply upright ears like Malinois, Dobies, and the big German shepherds that specialized in defense and attack. Sniffers were typically all floppy-eared. His dog was the only floppy-ear in sight.

Alex walked Valentin up to the line.

"Uh," Lieutenant Jurgen looked doubtful for the first

time. "Didn't design this course with a Russian bear dog in mind."

"Let's see how we do." Alex knew Valentin's ability even if the others didn't. His dog looked like he lumbered along, but he was so big that he covered ground surprisingly fast.

He was also smart as hell.

Alex hadn't been the only one watching Bethany and Trixie run the course.

At the line he said softly, "*Vperyod.*" Forward.

Valentin lumbered through the slalom line of stakes. They were so close-spaced that he had to take the time to turn almost ninety degrees for each passage, but he went through clean.

The tunnel was tight but he made it—sparing Alex the image of having to slice open the heavy culvert pipe to rescue his dog. The narrow walkway and high bridge were no challenge for his sure-footed dog.

Valentin took his "*Baryer!*" command and managed to Jump the four-foot wall with only a little difficulty. A hundred-and-eighty-pound dog was never intended to fly.

Alex could hear Carlton and a few of the other trainers making jokes about Valentin facing the six-foot wall further down the course.

Valentin glanced back to check in. Rather than calling aloud for an attack, Alex hand-signaled him to the truck.

All of the other dogs had jumped through the truck's window to put the bite on the mannequin. With his rear paws on the ground, Valentin simply rested his forepaws on the driver's windowsill, stuck his big head in—and ripped off the mannequin's head.

That silenced the other trainers.

"You can let him go around the wall," Jurgen commented as Valentin dropped his head and charged the six-foot wall.

But they'd come up with a tactic for that back in San Francisco.

At a full charge, Valentine turned sideways at the last moment and simply threw his shoulder into it. The fence exploded in splinters flying in every direction.

"Huh! Guess I'll have to make that a little stronger," was Jurgen's only comment.

Alex didn't tell him that the San Francisco course builders had gone through five generations of fences before they found one stout enough to stop Valentin.

The last task of the first lap of the course was to take down a "villain" in his monstrous bite suit.

Alex almost forgot; the padding was meant to protect the trainer from the bite of "normal" attack dogs. At the last second he let out a sharp whistle.

Valentin dug in his heels, slowing abruptly, and merely flattened the trainer. Rather than biting the trainer and risking the damage Valentin's massive jaws could cause through even the bite suit's padding, he simply sat on the trainer's chest. His massive tail flapped back and forth over the man's face mask, which probably made his helmet ring.

There was a round of applause.

Not from Carlton, of course.

Valentine clearly wanted to play some more. He

stared hard at Carlton for a moment to let him know when to be careful with his next comment, then called out "*Aport!*" Valentin stepped off the man in the bite suit, clamped his jaw on the shoulder padding, and trotted over, easily dragging the trainer with him.

The others' silence and Jurgen's thoughtful grunt was a sufficient praise for Alex.

## 2

——————

"This is utterly ridiculous!" Tanya leaned back against her desk with her arms crossed. "I have only just arrived in Washington."

"I have instructions from your father that if you refuse his order for your protection, I am to put you on airplane and send you home to Kyiv." Ambassador Tomas Khomenko stood at parade rest precisely three paces away, as he usually did when he was unhappy with his duty. Even in his advanced age, there was no taking the military out of the old soldier.

"Tomas!"

"Ms. Tatyana Ivanovna Larina." The ambassador was being stiffly formal, another bad sign.

"I can not go back. I have a treaty to sign."

"Yet, your father's order stands."

"He is only the Prime Minister. I was appointed to be Assistant Minister of Foreign Relations by the President, and approved by Parliament."

*Mostly* independent of her father's high position... Who was she fooling? But her appointment wasn't more than a quarter his doing. A third? But by God, the other two thirds had been all her. And this treaty would prove that she fully deserved the appointment. As herself, not her father's daughter.

"What say does he have over my life?" Apparently the power to still make Tanya feel like a petulant child of twelve instead of a woman in the prime of her life. She could protect herself; she was a trained soldier after all.

"Ms. Tatyana—" he sounded infinitely pained.

"Tomas!" He was so old school. It was as if he hadn't changed since the Soviet Union collapsed three decades ago.

"As you wish...Tanya." She didn't know if it was a good or bad thing that he appeared to choke on using the short form of her first name. Or that it pleased her so much at the moment.

"You've been Ukraine's ambassador to the US since long before Father became the Prime Minister. You could ignore him."

"I could. But the President, he has confirmed this protection order."

*Layno!* Shit!

"*Tak.* Yes. Fine. Bring in these *American* guards. I still do not know why I have need of them. I am very skilled." Despite her family's wishes, she'd served four years in the Ukrainian Ground Forces—joining the 95th Air Assault Brigade just before the War of Donbass. She'd been part of the historic strike four-hundred-and-fifty kilometers through Russian lines as they illegally grabbed the Crimea. Sadly, standing too close to a Russian tank she'd mined had cost her the use of her left ear and her service. But it had been beautiful watching the Russian tank die. Now she had a new way to serve.

"Thank you, Ms....Tanya. We do not know these American ways. We must keep you safe." He turned to go fetch the guards.

Anything to get her out of the Ukrainian Embassy. As self-important as the Americans were, they were *not* the center of Ukraine's world. Which was reflected in her country's Washington, DC embassy. Not only wasn't it on the main embassy row, it was the very farthest from the city center on the secondary row. Only Thailand, and Antigua and Barbuda were out this far.

The three-story brick edifice looked little better than a Soviet Khrushchyovka apartment block and was just as lacking in charm on the inside. Brown walls failed to accent the brown-linoleum flooring. Instead, combined with the narrow windows—steel-barred on the first floor —it required having the lights on even on a sunny afternoon, which failed to actually cast any warmth on the brown fake-leather furniture.

The ambassador had given her the nicest office after his own, which appeared to have had Joseph Stalin as the interior decorator. His bust had gone away on Ukrainian Independence Day in 1991 but nothing had replaced it— even Tomas looked like he'd been here since that day. There was a Ukrainian flag, and a picture of the Ukrainian President shaking her father the Prime

Minister's hand. She sighed. Even here she couldn't escape Father's watchful eye.

The only sign she wasn't in Kyiv was the white two-story Starbucks that faced the embassy from across the busy street.

Ambassador Tomas returned with two Americans... and their dogs. She hadn't expected that.

The first was a tall man, greatly bulked up by his bulletproof vest and all of the other gear hanging from his vest. He had no weapons, but he had the holsters, so his guns must be at the front security desk. He led in a Belgian Malinois as handsome as his master. The dog was scanning the room and sniffing the air while its handler was... scanning her. She had some experience with guard dogs, and far too much with men like him.

The second man was as different as possible from his companion. He was no heavier than the Malinois' handler, but he wasn't overwhelmed by his gear at all. He had one of those eternally young and hopeful faces. His expression was more the overeager boy than jaded urbanite. His hair was blond, and he wore a baseball cap with USSS across the brow in big letters. It was cocked just slightly askew, giving him a casual air.

His first action upon entering was to scan the room quickly. He barely looked at her, which was almost as irritating as the first man's blatantly assessing look. Then he snapped his fingers and waved one finger in a quick circle close by his side.

A massive Caucasian shepherd with a gorgeous dark brown coat padded out from behind him. The dog seemed to fill the room as he made a quick circuit of it—he crossed past file cabinets, around chairs, sniffed under her desk, and circled back around to the other side. His only pause was as he reached her. The big dog sniffed her, wagged his tail once, then moved on.

She'd been around enough Ukrainian Army guard dogs to know that wag was unusual. When they were seeking scent, trained dogs were very, very focused.

No one spoke until the dog had completed its circuit and returned to its handler's side.

"Show off."

She could just hear the Malinois' handler mutter to his teammate before he turned to her.

"Lieutenant Carlton Tibbets, ma'am, US Secret Service, Uniformed Division. I'll be leading your detail. This is Ripper." He neglected to introduce his companion.

"*Sidet'*," the blond agent spoke softly in Russian and the Caucasian shepherd sat beside him. He gave it a treat. Show off? Perhaps, but she also liked the thoroughness—trust nothing. The Russians had taught the Ukrainians *that* a thousand times over the centuries.

"Valentin, ma'am," he rubbed the dog's head, before looking up at her. "And I'm— Holy shit! Tatyana Larina."

The dog looked up at him in surprise and then turned to inspect her more closely.

"Tanya. I am to be called *Tanya*. Or better yet, Ms. Larina. *Not* that other name. Which should have been clear in one of your insidious American intelligence briefing files."

"I apologize for my language. Sorry, ma'am. And we weren't provided with any briefing file."

By Carlton's smug look, they had been and he'd chosen not to share it.

"But you are the spitting image," the unnamed agent continued.

"The spitting image of what?" But she was very afraid that she already knew his answer.

In a good Russian accent, he spoke the verse that was the bane of her existence. "*And so Tatyana was her name / Nor by her sister's brilliancy / Nor by her beauty she became / The attraction of every eye.*" He said it as more as a whisper than any arrogant recitation.

"What the hell?" Carlton was looking at his fellow agent.

It was from Aleksandr Pushkin's 1833 poetic masterpiece, *Eugene Onegin*. And she *was* the real-life twin of the most famous painting of Pushkin's fictional Tatyana Larina. She still hadn't forgiven her father for having the surname Larin then, knowing that, naming her after his favorite literary heroine, Tatyana. Being female, Larin became Larina.

Worse, Tatyana Larina was *not* Elizabeth Bennet with her happy-ever-after ending. Instead, Tanya was named for Russia's equally famous equivalent who had denied true love, instead choosing honor and duty in such a terribly depressing Russian way.

Her mother, where she'd gotten most of her looks, at least had the decency to see the irony. To this day, Father was still tickled by it.

Tomas was smiling with deep amusement, something

she hadn't known the man was capable of, despite his being a frequent guest at her family's dinner table when he was in the Ukraine.

"You shall *not* find me to be: *Wild, sad, silent did the maid appear / As in the timid forest deer,*" she replied in Russian with the next couplet of the poem.

Tomas' amusement grew, "That is a great truth."

She ignored them both and switched back to English. "Lieutenant Tibbets, do I need two dogs to guard me?"

"We'll be working in shifts. Based upon your profile—"

The Caucasian shepherd's handler twisted sharply at that. Carlton's smug smile returned. This Russian-speaking blond boy and his beautiful dog were not his favorites.

"—you are under possible threat from Russian agents. The treaty that you have sponsored—"

*Sponsored?* It had been her sole creation—ramming it through every step of the Ukrainian's arcane and corrupt political system.

"—is very unpopular with their government. We've been asked to protect you from potential foreign agencies until it is signed next week."

"And," the unnamed agent spoke up, his smile said it would be a tease, "it would look terrible if a high-ranking foreign official were to die on our soil." He had recovered quickly from his earlier surprise at not knowing about the report regarding her. Apparently, he was not even enough of a man to feel anger. If he were such a fan of *Onegin,* he should challenge this Carlton Tibbets to a duel over his besmirched honor.

And yet he looked at her as if he knew things about her just because she looked like a century-old portrait of a two-century old heroine.

Well, she'd show him that she was no cast member from Russia's Golden Age of Literature.

**3**

---

"Valentin, *Ko mne!*" To me. Tanya Larina called it out with the authority of someone who expected to be obeyed.

Valentin popped to his feet, and trotted over to her as she continued leaning back on the edge of her desk.

*What the hell?* Alex was so surprised the he couldn't even blink.

Russian bear dogs were suspicious of everyone and only ever answered to one master, the alpha dog—and Alex had done a lot of training to prove that was himself. The breed was always immensely loyal, but to *only* one master. They'd tolerate family and teammates, but never answer to them.

Yet Valentin trotted over to the Ukrainian beauty as if *she* was the alpha.

Granted, she was astonishing. Five-ten at least. Slender, the smoothness of her simple squat and how it left her well-poised to spring in any direction revealed advanced training—military or martial arts. Maybe dance, for which she certainly had the look.

Valentin nosed the long dark hair that slid forward off her shoulder in soft curls which echoed the Timoshenko portrait.

She gave Valentin a big hug and a head rub. His tail was wagging almost as fast as a Malinois'. He even licked her hand for crying out loud.

Valentin then turned to give him a look as if surprise that Alex hadn't accompanied him across the room.

"He is such a beautiful dog." Even though she didn't use a squeaky dog voice, Valentin was eating it up. Tanya's voice was low and smooth. And he could hear everything in her tone, the tease and the pleasure that her ploy had worked. But also the admiration for the great Russian bear dog.

But Valentin never socialized, especially not with other humans.

Apparently satisfied with having made her point, she stood.

Valentin remained close before her, looking up at her face.

"*Kysh,*" she wiggled her fingers at him. Shoo!

Valentin didn't move.

Alex considered calling Valentin back, but he knew what she'd done. Rather than confronting him over identifying her with Pushkin's tragic heroine, she'd tried to punish him by calling Valentin.

Alex wished he could ask his dog why that worked, but he wasn't going to help her get out of it unless she asked.

Besides, there was no denying the similarities. Her face was aristocratic, and she would look great in one of those early-1800s high-waisted empire-style dresses that cinched just below a woman's breasts. Though the stone-washed designer jeans and the red jewel-tone satin blouse did look exceptional on her as well. The lace-up mid-calf black boots kept her from appearing merely feminine. Instead she looked ready to take on some Russians.

She tried several things, until even Carlton was smiling, but Valentin was having none of it. She even tried ignoring him, but it was hard to ignore a waist-high, hundred-and-eighty-pound dog.

She finally looked from the dog to him. "What is the command I need?"

"Go Home," Alex said in English.

"*Domoy!*" She pointed at Alex's chest.

Valentin trotted back to stand at his side, but left a longing look in his wake.

"Thank you, Agent..."

"*Sergeant* Warren," Carlton answered for him. "Agent" meant protection detail, not Uniformed Division, but did he need to hit Alex's lower rank *quite* so hard?

"Alex Warren. That's how I got interested in Aleksandr Pushkin in the first place. We share part of a first name and a birthday."

"June 6th. Practically a national holiday—for Russians." Her tone reminded him that Ukraine was not Russia, though he knew Pushkin was almost equally popular there. He had been exiled to Odessa, Ukraine, while he wrote *Eugene Onegin,* after all.

"May 26th," Alex corrected her. "We overlap under the old style, Julian calendar that he was born under, not that new-fangled Georgian thing that the Soviets only adopted in 1918—along with the rest of the world, I'll admit."

Her eye roll was as emphatic as his parents' when he got on about Russian history. Nerd alert. Maybe he really should drop it.

"Are you first shift, Lieutenant Tibbets?" She very clearly turned the cold shoulder on him. *Real smooth, Alex. Way to impress the protectee.*

"Yes, ma'am. I'm with you until you lock down in your hotel tonight. Just tell me what time and Sergeant Warren will be waiting for you in the morning. Please do *not* leave your room unless he is there."

"Fine. Yes. I don't care. Let's get out of here." She pulled on a brilliantly blue parka but didn't bother zipping it against the DC cold—but he definitely felt a Ukrainian icy chill as she breezed by him and out the door. Carlton's sneer before he departed said that Alex had totally lost that round. Who knew what garbage Carlton would unload about him during his shift. If Alex found out that there was a single word against Valentin though, he'd—

"*Da.*" Ambassador Tomas Khomenko came up beside him.

Alex didn't even recall moving to the window. He watched her exit the embassy and walk down the street with her parka still open. Valentin had placed his front paws on the windowsill so that he too could watch her.

"You are going to be having troubles with that one,"

the ambassador continued.

"Lieutenant Tibbets is the head of the detail," he answered carefully.

"That is not of whom I was talking."

# 4

TATYANA BREATHED IN THE COOL AIR. IT WAS SO MUCH fresher here. Only February and the taste of spring was already on the air. Kyiv would still be wrapped in winter into April. DC also didn't have the heavy air pollution of Ukraine's capital. Instead, here the air tasted as if winter had never quite happened and crocuses were already nodding bright flowers above green grass.

Her choice to walk into DC's core, despite the embassy lying over two miles out, bothered Lieutenant Tibbets—he tried three times to direct her to one of the pair of black SUVs parked at the curb. She didn't care. Besides, his dog appeared to enjoy it as he took the lead, sniffing right and left as he went. Between the dog's aggressive attitude and the Belgian FN P90 submachine gun dangling across Carlton's chest, they cleared a hole down the sidewalk that she didn't have to think about walking through.

"You don't like your partner."

"What's to like?" Carlton seemed much more reasonable off by himself.

Good. Maybe she could rub him in Alex Warren's face for saying she was anything like her fictional namesake.

He continued, "He's from the West Coast, not DC. It may not sound like much, but they're slackers out there. We'd never have selected a Caucasian shepherd for a DC patrol."

"Yet both the Russian and Ukrainian armies have selected them as patrol dogs." Which made it even more surprising that her ploy had worked with Valentin.

Carlton nodded rather than arguing. "Yes, hyper-aggressive and hyper-loyal. However, that's not what makes a good ERT—Emergency Response Team—canine. We need high-speed, agility, and hair-trigger responses."

"Uh-huh." She wasn't really paying attention as they were passing the Nike store. She hadn't realized it was so close to the embassy. She definitely needed to get some cool runners before she returned to Ukraine. Maybe there was even a marathon to run here before she returned to Kyiv. Probably not in February. Americans were always so bothered by little inconveniences like cold.

"Do you run, Lieutenant Tibbets?"

"For sport? As little as possible. Do enough of it at work. My dog loves to run though, don't you, boy?" He said the last in a high cheery dog voice that made her think better of him.

His dog twisted to look at him in confusion.

"Sorry boy, I forgot you were working. *Such!*" He repeated the Seek command in German for his dog.

"Why doesn't he speak Dutch? Or even French?"

"Why would he do that?"

Tanya sighed. "Because he's a *Belgian* shepherd. Not a German shepherd. Very few Belgians speak German even as a second language."

"Oh," Carlton seemed to think she was serious. No sense of humor at all.

She did turn in at a Kate Spade store. She didn't mean to, but there was a satchel of a perfect spring green with matching leather handles hanging in the window that was utterly irresistible—so she didn't.

Carlton was tapping his foot impatiently by the time she came back out of the store, even though she'd been quick. Well, she'd taken a little time to choose between the tropical floral scarf and the blue dahlia one presently knotted around her ponytail.

They'd walked another block as she fussed with the new satchel. It was foolish to spend three hundred American dollars on a satchel she didn't really need, but she couldn't help smiling at it.

She was just considering if she should double back to the Nike store to challenge Carlton, when there was a sharp bark that made Carlton jump.

## 5

"Look at them jump! Well done. *Horosho! Horosho!*" Alex told Valentin. *Good! Good!*

He had hung back to get a briefing from the Ukrainian ambassador, since it was clear Carlton wasn't going to even show him the report that he'd been provided. *Asshole!*

Ambassador Tomas Khomenko had been more than obliging, offering succinct advice built on years of knowing Tanya Larina. It was clear that she was a headstrong woman used to having her own way—and not above baiting people. She'd already proven that with her summoning Valentin.

And it was impossible not to respect the man. Tomas' last days in the battlefield had been over thirty years before, but they'd included the Soviet-Afghan War. He was also very protective of Tanya on far more than a merely professional level. It meant Tomas liked her a great deal, which spoke to the woman and not just her governmental position.

Later, as he and Valentin had been driving back into DC, he'd spotted Tanya coming out of Kate Spade. Already impossible to miss, she had added a new green purse that stood out brighter than a Formula 1 car race start flag. He liked that flamboyance. The woman certainly had flair.

But, while Alex had waited and watched at a red light, he didn't like that Carlton had let Ms. Larina lag behind him as they moved down the street.

When he pulled even with them after the green light, he'd rolled down the passenger-side window so that Valentin could stick his big head out.

"*Govorit!*"

And Valentin had Spoken. Not a growl, which would be *Golos* or Voice, but a Russian bear dog-sized bark.

How Ripper didn't snap his own spine with how fast he turned was a testament to the flexibility of a Malinois. Carlton on the other hand had jumped beautifully...and had his FN P90 submachine gun more than half-raised before he'd stopped himself.

"Hey, buddy," he squeaked happily for Valentin's sake. "Remember to ignore me in the future when I tell you to surprise an armed Secret Service officer? Okay? Especially one who happens to be my new boss."

Valentin wagged his tail in answer with great thumps against Alex's shoulder as he kept his head outside. By protocol, Valentin was supposed to ride in back behind the cage screen, but where was the fun in that?

Alex twisted enough to glance through the tinted rear windows. Tanya looked as if she was laughing hard

enough to split a gut. Carlton looked ready to kill a bear...
or at least a Russian bear dog's handler.

Good on one front, but bad on another. He *really* had
to learn to think first.

Past 30th Street, they were almost to the Georgetown
Veterinary Hospital. Back in college, he could always spot
a library long before anyone else when he passed
through a town. And he knew the location of every used
bookstore within a hundred miles of San Francisco that
had even the tiniest Russian language collection.

Now, he could pick out every veterinarian emergency
clinic long before anyone else. Thank God Valentin had
never needed one, but he'd memorized all the big ones
and most of the smaller ones in DC during the drive east
just in case there was ever a need.

Close before the hospital, outside a coffee shop, were
an unlikely pair of men.

Alex wasn't sure why they were unlikely, but they
were and he'd been trained to trust that instinct.

He looked again, but they hadn't spotted him—
despite the massive dog head sticking out the passenger
window of a black, government-issued SUV.

No.

Their attention was locked down the block to the
west. Except they were being careful not to show it. Quick
glances, then turning away.

There was no line waiting to get into the coffee shop,
yet neither man held a to-go cup. Instead their hands
were jammed into their jacket pockets.

They might just be cold—the day hadn't warmed
much past freezing since this morning's workout at

JJRTC—and waiting for a friend. Or they might be clutching weapons.

A spot opened half a block up, and he pulled in as normally as he could, while not looking wholly away from the two men.

At his signal, Valentin followed him out the driver's side. They stayed to the street side of the parked cars. Here M Street was a busy four-lane plus packed parking on either side. Narrow shops in old two-story brick. They were bare brick or painted white, yellow, or gray. About every fourth building had a three-sided bay window jutting out into the sidewalk, including the vet hospital.

He was starting to draw ire from the drivers, so he quickly cut in between a Mercedes and a rusting Pontiac sedan—the only kind left—crossed the sidewalk, and got the veterinarian's bay window between him and the possible targets.

Through the bay, where someone was clutching a schnauzer as they sat in one of the waiting room chairs, he could see the backs of the two men. They still hadn't turned in his direction.

Down the block, Carlton and Tanya had started to cross the street to begin the coffee shop's block. Ripper was still scanning side to side, but Carlton had gone slack. It wasn't a big change in a Secret Service officer, but Alex knew the feeling. Too long on patrol. How pissed he was at the new guy from the West Coast. Or even just the momentary thought about how good a fresh cup of coffee would taste...or about the remarkably beautiful woman striding alongside him.

Whatever it was, neither he nor his dog had yet

twigged that they might be walking into a trap set half a block ahead.

Alex circled the bay window, signaling Valentin to heel closely, and came up behind the pair.

Having no leash to carry opened up his options. He casually rested his hand on the FN P90 across his chest as if steadying it. He also placed his other hand on the weapon he was most likely to use on a crowded city street: the butt of his taser.

At the last second, he had a crazy idea.

From a safe four paces back he called out in easygoing Russian, "Beautiful day, isn't it, guys?"

"*Da.*" One replied before turning to look at him. "*Der'mo!*"

*Shit! indeed, dude. Caught ya.*

His buddy turned, took one glance at the USSS emblazoned across Alex's vest, or perhaps it was the submachine gun, and echoed his buddy's curse.

Before Alex could take the next action, a pair of hipsters came out of the coffee shop clutching their afternoon lattes.

The two perps took advantage of the situation and dove into the coffee shop, slamming the door behind them.

The moment the hipsters were clear, he called out "*Aport!*" Fetch!

Valentin ran into the door—and bounced off the thick Lexan security glass, though Alex could hear the old wooden frame cracking.

His dog reared back to throw his shoulder into it.

Alex managed to reach over and twist the doorknob

just before Valentin struck. The door slammed open with a loud crash, but didn't shatter. Cries of surprise sounded inside.

He could see by the flurry that the two perps had bolted for the back.

He and Valentin were hot on their heels. Bolting under the flip-top counter, Valentin barely had to duck— he himself flipped up the countertop—past the three baristas that Valentin had brushed aside, and into the small rear prep area.

A manager was peeking out of a cubby office and just pointed in the direction the two men had run.

Alex had trained Valentin to hit the crash bar on metal doors, and it too slammed aside.

There were several cars double-parked in the small space off the alley. Cheap and old enough that they were probably the baristas' vehicles.

A hard squeal of tires, and he saw a white rental take off. He memorized the plate, but doubted if it would lead anywhere useful.

Ripper, closely followed by Carlton, raced into the near end of the alley just as the white rental shot out the far one. He was glad to see that Carlton had a hand firmly clenched around Tanya's arm, not leaving her behind to be someone else's target.

"Saw you go for them," Carlton puffed out as the three of them met under the alley's lone tree. The two dogs sniffed around, but the scent trail ended at the sharp black marks of the spinning tires.

"Two guys, watching your approach. Must be a third as a driver." Alex pulled out a radio and called in to the command center to mobilize District of Columbia police, search traffic cams, and start an immediate trace on the plate.

They promised him a call back quickly.

He turned to Tanya. "You okay, Ms. Larina?"

## 6

*WAS SHE OKAY?*

Tanya rubbed her arm where Carlton's hard grip had dragged her into a run.

Was she *okay*?

"Someone has just tried to kidnap me—"

She saw the glance between the two agents.

"—or worse. No, I'm *not* okay. *Ya rozlyuchenyy!*"

"What did she just say?" Carlton was looking at Alex.

"Not sure. It was Ukrainian, which only kinda carries over to Russian. Is *rozluychenyy* like *yarostnyy* or more like..."

"I'm pissed!" Tanya shouted in English.

"She's pissed," he told Carlton as if discussing the damned weather, then signaled his dog to return to his side.

The manager peered out the back door and Carlton went over to reassure him.

"There's something you should know," Alex said to her softly. "They spoke, and cursed, in Russian."

Tanya knew what that meant. *"Der'mo."*

"That's exactly what *they* said," he nodded after the car. "Like your new scarf, by the way. Really catches the blue of your eyes."

"Timoshenko's portrait had dark eyes." Though she had no idea why she was turning him back to that topic.

"True. But Liv Tyler in the movie has blue eyes. Your hair matches hers and the portrait's."

"The movie. I didn't even think of the movie." She groaned. But being compared to a movie actress who had modeled for Givenchy for over a decade made being upset difficult.

His phone rang.

*"Ohranyai!"* Alex told his dog as he pointed at her, then walked over to Carlton as he answered the phone.

Valentin sifted to full Guard mode, standing between her and the route the attackers had escaped by. He stayed on his feet and scanned the area. Ripper had returned to his master.

She rubbed Valentin's head for comfort. He sighed happily, but was no less vigilant.

Damn Father for being right. He'd said it was unsafe for her to come to Washington, DC a full week before the treaty signing. But she was *not* going to be some gilded bird in a cage!

Any alliance of Ukraine with the Americans was going to be bad for the Russians. Even worse for them, it was a trade alliance with the Turks as well. It was only a first step. If Ukraine could slowly work with the Turks, at first through the Americans before starting a more direct relationship, they could slowly tighten passage of the Bosporus Strait through Istanbul. If they did, it just might be possible to eventually have the Turks cut off the Russian's access from the Black Sea to the entire Mediterranean. Once that was achieved, then maybe the Russians would lose interest in the Crimea and it could once more be their own homeland. Then the Russians could be made to choke on the Don River and be restricted to their long, icy path to the Baltic.

It was just the first step in a very long endgame. But it was one she was glad to play. She would make them pay for the loss of so many of her comrades in the 95th Air Assault, of her hearing, and of the Crimea...pretty much in that order.

She must have worried the Russians more than she'd expected.

*Good!*

Worried enough to try and kill her?

Maybe *not* so good. It was something Russians tended to be very good at.

Carlton had clearly thought this was going to be some routine guard duty. Luckily for her, Alex had not.

But she'd be damned if she'd turn into some tremulous country maid afraid of her own shadow.

In all honesty, they didn't have reason to be *that* afraid of her. The chances of this actually working were very slim even if she had to try.

And how had the Russians known she'd chosen to walk? Because she often did, even in Kyiv winters...or because someone had told them.

A lookout on the street?

A Russian sympathizer at the embassy? She'd alert Tomas and he'd get to the bottom of it, if that was the problem.

Carlton had been with her.

But why had Alex been so far behind them?

She'd taken over half an hour with her walking and window shopping to come this single kilometer from the embassy. Her goal today had been to get the lay of the land and see the American capital. She'd go to work tomorrow.

Had Alex perhaps taken time to call in a couple of his buddies to lurk and then be chased off? Some arrogant male showoff trick to put his partner down? Did their escape from a Russian bear dog seem that likely? They'd only been a few steps away from Alex when they dashed into the storefront. Carlton had dragged her around the corner before she could see how quickly—or slowly— Alex followed.

Maybe Carlton was right and Sergeant Alex Warren lived to a different standard.

When he and Carlton returned from their phone call, she ignored Alex.

"Well? What did they learn?"

Carlton answered. "The car went missing from the Embassy of New Zealand this morning. They dumped it six blocks from here and disappeared. These guys were pros and knew right where the traffic cams were. All we ever got were the backs of their heads. One went into Trader Joe's, a grocery store, another strolled into the

Westin hotel lobby and disappeared, the last one may have taken the subway."

Okay, perhaps it wasn't something that Sergeant Alex Warren had arranged on a whim. But he still had to answer for calling her Pushkin's tragic heroine.

## 7

---

"WELL, I FOUND A HELL OF A LOT OF WAYS TO PISS OFF OUR fearless leader on my first day."

Bethany had called him up and offered to drag him out for a welcome-to-DC beer. To offset today, Alex probably needed five or six.

They met at seven at a packed bar called the Wet Dog Tavern a mile or so north of the White House. She'd said to bring his dog. The owners had been charmed...and Valentin's sheer size had won them a corner table.

The instant Alex saw Flying Dog's UnderDog gold lager, he'd ordered it. A beer named to fit his foul mood. It would be perfect, except he actually liked the beer.

Valentin was now sprawled at his feet, fast asleep. To finish off the afternoon, they'd gone for a long run around the Mall and through the first layer of back streets for familiarization.

On their arrival here at the tavern, his dog hadn't cared about Bethany or her dog at all. Even after two weeks working together in San Francisco, Valentin had grown no closer to either one. Not a threat? Not a problem. That was his apparent assessment. Very different from his reaction to Tatyana Larina.

Trixie curled up in a neat ball, carefully not too close to Valentin, and watched him intently rather than sleeping. She clearly remembered the bear dog's hard growl from this morning.

"Yeah, you two did a number on poor old Ripper this morning out at JJRTC. Carlton was so stirred up; he gave that poor dog half the signals wrong." And had earned their team the lowest course score of the day. Bethany was very amused, even if her dog still looked worried.

"Then we missed the perps," Alex just couldn't seem to stop grinding over each misstep in his head. "Really not a good day. Captain Baxter was not pleased." He'd spent a long hour in the White House Secret Service room in the West Wing. He'd never been to the White House, but all he saw was the guarded door to the Situation Room and the tight-packed cubie-land occupied by the USSS. Baxter had grilled him on every detail and every second of the encounter, right down to having Valentin "speak" at Lieutenant Carlton Tibbets.

"He's never pleased, by anything." Bethany had not ordered an UnderDog. She'd gotten a Kona's Big Wave lager as if she was riding high. Really easy to picture her as an ultra-fit blonde surfer gal—she had the look down even in DC-winter gear. Of course, being from West Virginia made that assessment unlikely.

"Certainly not by me." When she offered, they tasted each other's beer. Hers was all bright with life and hope.

She'd merely said, "Nice" about his rather than some deserved remark on UnderDog's total appropriateness.

"One of the other pointy-ears..."

Handlers were identified by their dogs.

"...thinks that they *found* Baxter when they originally dug out the West Wing Basement. He says that they must have built the USSS offices right around him. Baxter takes his White House dogs very seriously."

"But I'm not a White House dog. I'm Uniformed Division."

"Baxter doesn't care. He's technically head of White House UD, not for all of DC, but he doesn't care. You're in DC, you handle a dog, you're his."

Alex stayed with the dogs and studied his beer while Bethany went and fetched their burgers. The bar didn't have a kitchen, but instead had a tiny independent burger stand in the corner. The guy offered just three different burgers, and all they came with was potato chips. Didn't matter.

Carlton hadn't been happy about him making the play on his own. But if he'd called to Carlton, what would he have done? Exposed his protectee even more?

Baxter hadn't been happy that he hadn't called for backup. As if there'd been time.

And Tatyana Larina appeared to just be pissed at him in general...somehow blaming him for the bad scrape he'd pointed out on her brand-new purse.

"Hell of a first day," Bethany said as she dropped their plates on the table. Four of them, two with fully dressed burgers and chips and two with just patties. "Maybe these will cure that sour look."

"They're all mine?" Because they did smell damn good.

"Dream on, West Coast." Then she shoved over one of two plates with just a patty on it. She set hers in on the floor for Trixie and he did the same for Valentin.

Valentin woke up long enough to swallow his—he didn't appear to even bite it. Trixie at least took two or three bites before licking her lips and looking around to see if more burgers were falling from heaven.

"You're a good person, Bethany Wilson."

"That's *Sergeant* Wilson to the likes of you." She smiled as she bit into her burger.

He matched her.

*Damn.* Seriously good. A beer and a good burger with a knock-out blonde dog handler. His mood was getting better already.

"And don't get that look."

"What look?" Did he have a look?

"You might be ever so purdy, but you're not my type," Bethany mumbled around a mouthful of burger.

"What *is* your type?" Because she was hella cute. Even if he was thinking of a certain Ukrainian... *No!* He so was *not* doing that.

"You got a mirror?"

"Not with me."

"Next time you find one, look in it."

"And..." he prompted when she didn't continue.

This time her smile was evil. "Then you'll see what's not my type."

Dogs. He understood dogs. He'd stick with that.

Then he looked down at Valentin and recalled how

43

his notoriously standoffish companion, even by Russian bear dog standards, had looked at him reproachfully this afternoon when he'd called him off guard duty and returned to his truck without Ms. Larina.

Nope. He didn't understand dogs either.

At least the burger was good and the beer seemed to fit. UnderDog—just bloody perfect.

# 8

Tanya scowled out through the peephole of her hotel room door.

She'd be damned if she'd cower behind a door until the Secret Service decided it was about damned time to show up, no matter what Carlton had said last night.

The clerk at Kate Spade had offered to send the purse back to the manufacturer to see if they could fix it, but it would be at least a week. She was supposed to be back in Ukraine in a week. So now she had a damaged purse, which also added to her feeling of no good cheer.

That and the Russians had decided to attack her.

Well, she'd had arranged a little visit from the Ukrainian embassy armorer to her hotel room last night —without Carlton or Ambassador Tomas looking over her shoulder. If the Russians wanted her, they'd best come prepared to take some losses.

Where was that man? Probably off writing some dated romantic poetry, just dripping with Russian heartache dredged up from too much cheap vodka and salty chechil cheese.

She'd even worn her new Natalia Romanova-designed dress that she'd picked up during Ukraine Fashion Week. She did it just to grind her heel into his face that she wasn't his demure-and-proper Pushkinesque heroine.

Sick of waiting, she yanked open her room's door, strode out into the hall, and slammed into the opposite wall when she tripped over the great Russian bear dog lying across her threshold.

"You okay?"

Tanya retrieved her leather jacket from the floor. Then she did her best to rearrange her clothes before she turned to look down at Sergeant Alex Warren sitting against the wall beside her door.

Valentin was watching her with a happy smile of greeting.

"Don't worry, you can't hurt him with a little kick like that. His mother may have been a T-84, but his father was a T-14 Armata."

The T-84 was Ukrainian's finest tank, but the T-14 was Russia's newest and gave her chills when she imagined one rolling along her country's roads at eighty kilometers an hour.

Alex sat cross-legged on the plush red hallway carpet —ornate enough to be Russian—with a pad and pen in his hands.

"What drivel are you writing?"

He looked down at his hands in surprise, then back

up at her. "A letter to Mom. She's an old-school lawyer and prefers the written word over email."

"It had better not be about me."

He held up the pad in front of his eyes, though it was clear he wasn't reading whatever was written there.

"Dear Mom, All that schooling in Russian literature that you and Dad so despised has finally paid off." He paused and looked up at her. "They're very practical people, Mom and Dad. Both career lawyers. Anyway... The woman of Pushkin's Russian dreams has become my Ukrainian reality. Fairer than a dawn breeze, which, sadly for the sake of this metaphor, it isn't especially warm in DC right now—which also makes it an *accurate* metaphor. Despite her chill demeanor, she's wearing an absolutely killer dress that matches her dark and mysterious eyes." He looked up at her again. "Sorry for taking liberties with your eye color, but it reads better on the page. Have you ever considered dark contacts?" Alex cleared his throat and returned his attention to his pad. "There's a fairytale-like air to her that—"

She prepared to kick him with the sharp toe of her Manolo Blahnik boots.

"Or maybe you aren't interested." He tucked the pad away.

"How long have you been sitting here?"

"I came on shift at seven. You hadn't called yet, and Valentin wanted a chance to shed all over this pretty carpet—it is spring soon and he's already dropping his undercoat in great wads of fur—so we came here. The temperature is up in the forties today. You shouldn't freeze in the dress, which really is absolutely killer on you by the way."

Carlton had said nothing about calling in her morning schedule. Alex had been sitting over an hour because he and his boss were acting like children. Fine. Let him.

"I'm hungry. Let's go."

"You said the magic word. *Yeda!*" Valentin responded with enthusiasm at the mention of Food! They both clambered quickly to their feet.

Tanya led off down the long hall, or tried to. She made it three steps before Valentin pushed past her to take the lead.

At first she thought that he was going after a half-finished breakfast of eggs and bacon that someone had set outside their door. Though he sniffed at it, he didn't stop.

"You must feed him a great deal for him not to take that."

When she glanced, Alex was hanging just a step back. Rather than watching her ass as she'd expected, he was watching over his shoulder as someone came out of their room farther down the hall.

"Well, he had a half-kilo of raw beef and a bowl of steamed veggies this morning, though a Caucasian shepherd would happily eat itself obese if allowed. But first, he's on the job, and second, he accepts nothing except from my hand. Food safety. Security dogs are a target."

"Whoever would hurt a sweet dog should be shot!"

"Amen, sister!" Alex's light words didn't match his dark tone.

The tone surprised her. Alex had seemed so light and facile—a uniformed officer quoting Pushkin in the original—yet he was the one who had identified and chased her would-be attackers. And as they spoke, he still kept an awareness of their surroundings. Completely on the job.

She had to remind herself of what Tomas had said, *American Army dog handlers are feared in all war zones, they have heavy bounties on their heads. And the Secret Service handlers do this in broad daylight instead of under the cover of night. The American protection details are one of the most elite and bravest forces anywhere.*

Even if Alex and Carlton did act like children.

Once they reached the polished copper of the elevator doors, she observed their reflection as they waited. The guard, the woman in the body-skimming white lace dress, and massive dog who had squeezed in between them.

Natalia Romanova had cut the dress for Tanya herself. The inner sheath reached from her shoulders to mid-thigh. The thick lace flower-work also covered her arms to her wrist, up her neck higher than a turtleneck, and down to stop just above her knees. *You have the legs for me to cut it shorter, even more than most women can wear.* But Tanya had insisted on the more conservative look for meetings—fashion forward but not showing the skin she normally would.

Even with the longer cut, it would be a little chilly, but

she'd needed the fashion statement to gather her nerves for today's meetings.

The white lace paired with the charcoal boots and sixty-millimeter peg heels combined to say, "I'm serious, but I'm glad to kick ass too." The boots also made her several centimeters taller than Alex. If it bothered him, he made no sign of it.

She slid on the hip-long black bomber jacket she'd found at Fashion Agony. The only colors were her blue eyes and her green Kate Spade satchel. As planned.

Alex was right though; it was a killer look.

And it would be perfect for all the meetings today as she began her campaign to maneuver the Turks and the other Black Sea Balkans into freeing the Crimea from the Russians over the next few years. And she didn't mind for a moment that the best place to wage her campaign was in this American city. The Americans knew how to live in ways no Ukrainian could.

Maybe tonight she'd go dancing.

She eyed their reflections. Did Alex dance?

## 9

It wasn't just a long day; it was a *damn* long day. Maybe going for a run *before* he'd begun his shift hadn't been his best idea.

One look at Valentin and Alex knew that wasn't the problem.

Yes, in addition to a positive attitude, Russian bear dogs had incredible stamina. But that was an area where he and his dog usually matched.

Valentin looked as if he'd gladly keep going—especially if Tanya was involved. She'd acted like a supercharger on Alex's typically complacent companion.

Alex would shoot himself if he had to do more.

Assistant Foreign Minister Tanya Larina had turned into a whirling dervish.

Breakfast was a bagel with cream cheese during her first business meeting with a Ukrainian attaché. Her second meeting was also over breakfast where she didn't stint either, consuming black coffee and two eggs, toast, and sides of both bacon and sausage. She also ate some poor sub-assistant to the Secretary of the US Navy alive over the meal. As they left that meeting, she'd grumbled.

"The next meeting, it will not be such a waste of time." She'd extracted a promise of a meeting with the Under Secretary from the poor assistant.

All day she clawed her way up the food chain. He'd lost track of how many meetings they'd gone to...before lunch.

His routine throughout the day had followed protocol: escort, inspect the room, then fade into the background.

As she tucked into a large lunch at a Chinese restaurant with a spook from the Bulgarian embassy, he began to wonder how she kept her amazing figure. Even with the high-necked dress, most men were having trouble not staring at her body. So much so, that none of them noticed the sharp mind carving them up like a butcher's knife.

By the two o'clock handover to Lieutenant Carlton Tibbets, Alex knew how she kept her figure—because she *never* slowed down. Not for a single instant.

If they had ten minutes walking between meetings, he'd get a download of everything that had gone wrong.

At first he'd thought that she was the epitome of a Slavic pessimist. But over time he understood that she drove herself hard, and even the smallest misstep needed to be second-guessed and rethought before the next meeting. Her drive was relentless, so relentless that he was wrung dry just trying to keep up with her.

She didn't expect him to just listen to her self-debriefs—she expected him to participate. He'd spent the last two years walking a dog and five years with the Service before that. His job was more complex than that, but being a dog handler meant dealing with immediate information. Here and now scenarios. Short-term attack vectors. Protection routes and strategies. The furthest he ever thought ahead was during route planning.

But to satisfy Tanya's insatiable need to understand, he'd had to dredge up his decade-gone past. It took a surprising amount of effort to reach back into the history that had been the cultural backdrop of 19th Century Russian Romanticism. Strategies of the five tsars of Russia and the five sultans of the Ottoman Empire came slowly back to mind, but some of their strategies and maneuverings seemed to help Tanya.

Doing that, while remaining on full alert, and keeping a constant check on Valentin had wrung him dry.

Tanya Larina was a political animal, a world he knew almost nothing about. She played move and countermove scenarios across a span of years. Which, with the volatile short-term nature of Ukrainian politics, was pretty damn ballsy.

Once she dragged Tibbets off in whatever the next direction was, Alex reported in. Nothing new on yesterday's three assailants. Nothing for today except to turn his log entries into a briefing report that no one would ever read...unless something went wrong. Then every word and each random typo would be scraped over with a threshing machine guaranteed to mangle the author of said report. He considered writing it in Russian to further recover that part of his memory but decided that might not be the best choice for a US government report.

When he finally got back to the apartment complex, he considered knocking on Bethany's door and seeing if she wanted to split a pizza. She'd found him an empty townhouse just three doors down from hers. The place was dog friendly, especially Secret Service dog friendly, which was a major bonus. He could also afford it. One bedroom upstairs, living and kitchen below. It fit him just fine.

Then he figured that if Bethany was around and did say yes, he'd probably end up talking about the wild politician woman who had been unleashed on an unsuspecting Washington, DC. And he'd learned long ago that the last thing a woman wanted to hear about was another woman—even if he *wasn't* Bethany's type.

Instead, he walked softly by, slipped into his own place, and grimaced at the piles of boxes. It was mostly books—in Russian. Very few of them had been published after 1900. But first he had to assemble the bookcases. However, when packing, he'd dropped the bag of shelf hardware into one of the book boxes...without marking which one. And if he began opening boxes, there wouldn't be any space to assemble the bookcases to put the books on.

*Screw it!* He'd been in Washington for all of three days. They could wait.

Valentin waded through the morass as if it was just another training course. He flopped down in front of the sliding glass doors and sighed contentedly. It was the only clear floor space, and Valentin had already learned that the morning sun shone right there.

Except today they'd been up and gone before the seven-a.m. sunrise. Tomorrow, too.

Alex's sofa still had a blanket and pillow, but no sheets. And it wouldn't matter if he did have the sheets, because he'd lost the hardware for the bed frame. He had a niggling feeling that it was still sitting in the corner of his old closet...in San Francisco.

"Moving sucks, Valentin."

Valentin snored at him in response.

He checked his watch, six-thirty p.m. and almost full dark.

Yeah, so done. He called for a pizza and caught a quick shower.

In the mirror he asked himself what *was* Bethany's type?

But his mind twisted the question and asked what was Tatyana Larina's?

Bethany was the true all-American girl. Beautiful, athletic, talented girl-next-door looks—almost literally girl next door as she lived just down the row.

Tanya, despite her protests, drew him the way the Russian heroines had, from Pushkin's Tatyana Larina to Tolstoy's Anna Karenina born half a century later. Amazing, driven women, trapped by circumstances outside their control.

Curiously, he had followed in their footsteps, after a fashion. In pursuing the unexpected, he'd forged his own path away from the family's law firm. The eighth generation?

Not him. His sister had fought the bit, and lost. Now she was San Francisco's most ruthless family lawyer—with a vicious side that he barely recognized from their youth.

But she was also his only supporter in following his own path. "Hold out as long as you can, Alex."

Listening to Tanya Larina throughout the day, he could see that she too was forging her own blazing path across the political landscape. *That* was even more attractive than her beauty.

At a knock on his door, he dragged on jeans and a USSS t-shirt, the only clean things he had handy, and hurried back downstairs.

He fished out his wallet and opened the door.

"You weren't going to eat pizza without me, were you?" And there was Bethany with a pizza in one hand, two beers in another, and a dog on her heels.

"Hell no, woman. I'm not crazy enough to try and do that." He held the door wide and waved her in.

Valentin raised his head eagerly, saw who it was, and flopped back out of sight with a soft growl of displeasure.

"Most pleasant greeting yet. Guess I'm making headway." Bethany stepped in and he had his wallet half tucked away. "Hey! Keep that out. You owe me twenty."

He pulled out a twenty and jammed it in her back pocket as she turned for the kitchen.

She sent him a dangerous look.

Then it struck him what he'd just done. Yeah, just one of the guys, so shove the money in her pocket. Except Bethany was a her and he'd just put his hand on her ass.

"Shit! Sorry. I didn't mean to— Shit!"

"Not my type, remember? Just watch them hands, bub."

"Yes, ma'am. Sorry about that. I—"

"Shut up, Cisco Kid."

"Yes, ma'am."

"Shee-it!" She gave it a good West Virginia drawl. Then she looked at the train wreck of his boxes. "Any idea where some plates are hiding?"

He tore the flap off the nearest box, ripped it in two, and handed one to her.

"Yeah, close enough."

While she served the pizza, he stripped the blanket and pillow off the couch and kicked two boxes into place as side tables. One *tinked* as if he'd probably just broken one of his few plates. The other almost broke his toe, which meant the box was filled Russian literature with an attitude.

## 10

"Do you dance?" A woman's voice on the phone asked him in Russian. Tanya Larina.

"Do I...dance?"

Bethany was looking at him strangely. They'd finished most of the pizza and both beers. Now they were at either end of the couch and talking about dogs. Big surprise there. He'd managed to avoid the protectee topic, mostly.

"*Da. Ya tantsuyu,*" was all Alex could think to say.

"Good. Your Lieutenant Carlton Tibbets does not run and I can not imagine that he dances. Is he even alive? My day is over and I need to drop it in the road. Leave your dog and pick me up in fifteen minutes. We are going dancing." And she hung up.

He put his phone away and ran his hand through his hair, trying to figure out what had just happened.

"What's up?" Bethany still sat on the end of his couch.

"Uh," he wasn't sure. It *was* his job to provide protection duty. And that meant he was on call. But...

He didn't have anything to place on the other side of that. Tanya's safety was his job.

He checked his watch. Nine-thirty at night. Tomorrow he was on duty at seven.

His protectee had just made it sound as if she was going out with or without him. He was actually impressed that she had called him at all. Yesterday's attack must have spooked her more than she was willing to admit. But she also wasn't going to let such a thing keep her from doing what she wanted.

"Uh," he looked at Bethany again, then shrugged. "Looks like I'm back on duty." He checked his watch again. "Actually, I'm already late." Because even if he hit all the lights green, he was twenty minutes from her hotel.

"Welcome to the friggin' Secret Circus," Bethany pushed to her feet and scooped up the last piece of pizza. "Ain't protection detail just so fine?" She walked out the front door.

He hit his gun safe and pulled out a slimline radio along with two concealed carry pieces.

He had the feeling it was going to be a long night.

## 11

TANYA WAS WAITING WHEN A BRILLIANT-YELLOW, FOUR-door Jeep Wrangler Moab pulled up to the door of the Fairmont hotel and stopped close in front of her.

A valet opened the passenger door for her.

"Let's walk." Though if there was a proper ride, in her opinion this was it.

Alex looked at her across the empty seat. "Let's not."

"Why?"

"Because without Valentin along, I want something big to run over the bad guys with."

"Let's walk anyway."

Alex just shook his head. "Without Valentin, I'm going to limit attack vectors. That doesn't include exposing you unnecessarily. You shouldn't have even walked through the hotel lobby."

She actually liked that he insisted. So many of the men during her day had been pushovers. Their jobs were to block her from reaching their superiors, just like any bureaucrat's. None had succeeded. Yes, these had been all low-level meetings, but she'd managed to arrange meetings with next-level people in every case.

Not one had the spine to stand up to her. Not one had challenged her.

Even Carlton she'd been able to whipsaw back and forth...a little.

He also had no understanding of politics.

She climbed up into Alex's top-of-line Wrangler. A hundred-thousand euro in Ukraine, here in the United States it was just another SUV—one that fit her idea of what one should be. It was easy to image exploring the backroads of America. In warmer weather, take the top down, the doors off, and race away from her cares with the wind blowing through her hair. She could definitely imagine that as a lifestyle.

Alex had done more than stand up to her. She hadn't noticed how helpful he was between meetings until he was off-duty and Carlton had replaced him.

"How do you know so much about Ukrainian politics?"

He shifted into gear and headed northwest across DC to the address the concierge had given her.

"I don't. But I know Russian politics from the nineteenth century. I studied the literature against the backdrop of the Russian Empire that existed from Catherine the Great until the Soviet purges. The Crimean War, the first one, was right at the heart of the Golden Age of Russian literature and altered its shape in fascinating ways that carried on for decades after the 1856 defeat of... Sorry. I get a little stupid on this subject."

Tanya considered his words as he drove in silence.

Alex's insights had been helpful when she'd been thinking about the Balkans along the west of the Black Sea. But they'd been even more useful after her meetings with the Turks—the progeny of the Ottoman Empire who had led the fight against the old Russian Empire during the Crimean War. He didn't know the current politics, but he understood the underlying dynamics of each people's pride and power as clearly as her father.

Her father would like this man. There was a thought.

If only Alex wasn't so irritating.

She thumped her head against the padded headrest as they rolled up in front of the DC9 club.

Was he irritating because her father *would* like him? He'd clearly shared Father's pleasure for her Pushkinesque name. If that was part of the problem, she needed to do some thinking. Because if anyone knew what drove her, it was her father. Her mother always sighed when the two of them started on politics because they were so obviously of the same mind. No matter how fierce their debates became, they were over tactics and strategies, not underlying policies.

She wasn't paying attention until Alex had parked and circled to open her door.

Sitting in the Jeep, she just looked at him. He was handsome in a remarkably blond-American way. Smart and good at his job—if she ignored his boss' comments.

Yes, she could do far worse.

Ukrainian men knew who she was, and they cared deeply about *that*. In her foolish youth, she'd thought it was about her. In time she'd learned that dating the

Prime Minister's daughter was an obvious path to a bright future. It had made her drop many men on the road. Now her choices were taken with much more care.

Sergeant Alex Warren would have no such agenda.

Yes, tonight she would have fun.

## 12

"TANYA? YOU OKAY?"

She gave him an odd look, which he should be used to by now. Tanya Larina was one of the least predictable women Alex had ever been around.

Bethany was sharp, funny, and had a shield wall about a mile high.

Tanya's emotions never showed in a meeting. Afterward all of the doubts and questions traveled across her face in a fascinating sequence.

But he hadn't seen a look quite like the one that shifted onto her face as she inspected him while he continued holding the Jeep's door open for her.

Except it wasn't really her door.

It was usually…Valentin's!

He looked down at her knee-length, white-wool coat and swore.

She arched her eyebrows at him in question.

"Uh. Valentin usually sits there. I didn't brush off the seat before you sat down. I'm so sorry. I have a lint brush.

Somewhere." At the apartment in some unknown box. "I—"

She squinted at him, then down at the seat she still sat in. "I did say to leave your dog home."

"I left...most of him home," Alex did his best to smile. "At least the part that drools and barks."

"But not the part that sheds."

Alex sighed. "Not the part that sheds."

"That is easy to take care of." She shrugged out of the coat though the temperature was back down near freezing and stepped out of the Jeep.

He attempted to apologize once more, but didn't manage it.

The lovely white lace dress, that earlier had been suitable for an updated Tatyana Larina, had been replaced. Now she wore cobalt blue leather. Short-sleeved top, a heart-stoppingly shorter skirt, and a deep-V cleavage that only a slender woman like her could get away with. Unless he missed his guess, it might be backless as well.

She ran a finger across his chest, underlining the USSS logo on his t-shirt.

"Best clothes I've got," he did his best to recover though her touch had distracted him—badly. He scanned the street again to make sure nothing had changed other than his blood pressure.

"As they have already saved my life once, I'm inclined to agree. Let's dance."

Alex tossed his jacket in the Jeep, locked it, and escorted her to the entrance of DC9.

## 13

TANYA TOSSED BACK A STOLI VODKA WHICH LIT A FIRE DEEP in her belly. She didn't sip it because she didn't want to get drunk. She wanted the heat.

Actually, she wanted to have an excuse for the heat she was already feeling.

The Regrettes was a garage-funk-punk rock-or-something band with three female leads and a male drummer. It didn't matter what they were, they'd burned up the stage with two hours of totally danceable music without even a breath between songs. The DC9 hall was packed with the young people of Washington, DC dancing as hard as at any Ukrainian disco.

Alex didn't just dance, he danced well. Very well, which was the real cause of the heat coursing through her. She'd expected a merely fun evening. But Alex was a man who knew how to lead, how to make any dance snap with tension until it felt like they were having sex on the dance floor.

And it wasn't just the dancing that was adding to the fire.

Without once missing a step, he was always looking around the room.

At first, she'd thought that maybe he was watching the other women, because there were a lot of them and many...some...a few were dressed as high-end as she was. Most of those *had* hit the slut button and it seemed to attract every male's eye. With the fifteen-centimeter tall "USSS" emblazoned across the back of his t-shirt, he certainly gained a lot of attention himself.

But it wasn't the darkness or strobing of the lights that made him never focus on any particular woman. In fact, he spent more time watching the men. Assessing the competition?

No, he was doing the same thing she was—assessing possible threats.

They were dancing their hearts out, and *still* he was on guard, watching for breaks in the patterns of the crowd or something. For her it came from paranoia, but for him it was vigilant duty.

That was *very* attractive.

By the time the first slow-dance number came up, she hadn't even hesitated, just stepped into his arms. There was a safety there. He guided her expertly, so that they didn't bump a single couple despite the crowded floor. But he also kept turning them slowly as if it was completely natural, shifting through the crowd with a calm ease that would make them hard to pin down as a target.

She'd finally just let herself go and trusted to his

skills. Instead she focused on appreciating the physical man as well as the protective one. He might not be as robustly muscular as his dog was, but she could feel that Alex Warren was whip strong. And after they'd sweat enough that he no longer smelled of soap, he'd become deliciously male.

He was not some Russian-speaking professorial type. He was a United States Secret Service agent, which meant he was also an elite warrior.

In Alex's arms, that was now impossible to ignore.

However long had it been since...Sergey? Or was it Yegor who she'd been with most recently? Whoever, it had been too long.

The fire of the vodka after the heat of dancing made her just let go.

"Come on. It's time." She grabbed his hand and dragged him toward the door.

The chill of the night air as they walked to his Jeep didn't feel cold at all. After the heat of the dance hall, it felt wild and fresh.

"You are coming back to the hotel with me," she informed him as he held her door and she climbed back into the Jeep.

"I...what? No."

She closed the door in his face.

He circled around and climbed in the driver's side. "Besides, I left Valentin at home."

"Fine, we will go there then."

"No, Ms. Larina. That's not going to happen."

"I will scream bloody murder if you try to remove me from this vehicle at my hotel."

He glared at her, still not starting the engine. "Are you always this much trouble?"

"You must ask my father that someday."

She laughed as he made a strangled sound, but he started the engine and drove off.

## 14

A<small>LEX</small> <small>ACTUALLY</small> <small>HAD</small> <small>HIS</small> <small>KEY</small> <small>IN</small> <small>THE</small> <small>APARTMENT</small> <small>DOOR</small> before he came to his senses.

"Uh, you can't come in."

"Because it isn't right?" Tanya asked in disdainful Russian.

"Well, it isn't," he stuck with English. "But that's not the only problem."

She pushed him aside and turned the key. "Why? Do you have another woman in there?"

"No, I..." Alex gave up.

Tanya opened the door and stepped in. Then burst out laughing.

"Okay, so I haven't really had a chance to unpack yet. Think of it as early U-Haul decor."

"You are bohemian?"

At the sound of her voice, Valentin popped his head up, leapt over the boxes faster than an obstacle course training, and practically slammed into her with his eagerness to greet her.

He knew the reference Tanya meant, of course. Not America's bohemian beatniks of the 1950s and '60s, but the marginalized and starving artist culture of 1800s France.

Was he?

Before the Secret Service, he certainly had been—except for the family money which he'd refused to touch other than for tuition. Instead of living at home while attending UC Berkeley, he'd rented a typical student garret except for his junior year abroad in St. Petersburg. It had been very bohemian and he'd enjoyed it far more than the familial showpiece.

Alex delayed his answer by greeting Valentin, then nudging him back so that they could close the door.

There was little question about what he *wasn't* supposed to be doing with a protectee.

Valentin pushed forward again.

Tanya tossed her be-furred coat over a box before squatting down to greet Valentin—who was eating it up like, well, a puppy dog. The two of them had some crazy connection, like siblings or something. The Pushkin poem had never said anything about Tatyana Larina having a great hound—though, being a member of rural Russian aristocracy, she probably had. Was Valentin in some weird way the dog Tanya had owned in a former, fictional life?

Or maybe he just enjoyed the feel and smell of her.

His own body remembered what hers had felt like in his arms. Tatyana Larina might be a foreign diplomat, but she was also an incredibly fit and lovely woman.

She rose from hugging Valentin and ended up

standing practically nose to nose with him in the tiny front entryway.

"I am not some fantasy out of your Pushkin novel."

He breathed her in like a heady scent. No, she wasn't some arcane model of duty and decorum. She was incredibly alive.

"I'm going to regret this in the morning."

She draped an arm over either of his shoulders and clasped her hands behind his neck. "I won't."

He shifted her two steps back until she was out of the entryway and had her back against the cool metal of the stainless-steel fridge, empty except for some dog meat.

She was right.

If he was going to go to hell, he was damn well going to enjoy it.

## 15

"YOU MUST DO SOMETHING ABOUT YOUR BED." THOUGH Tanya couldn't imagine why she was complaining, she felt incredibly limber this morning.

She sat on the bathroom counter, drying her hair as well as she could with a couple of kitchen towels, and watched Alex drying himself off with a stack of paper napkins bearing a pizzeria's logo. He was a very pretty lover as well as being a very creative one.

They'd made use of the kitchen floor, had something of a wrestling match on the carpeted stairs that had ended with two victors, and finally shoved around enough boxes to get the mattress flopped down upstairs.

They'd prowled through boxes of Russian literature, dog care books, and action-adventure thriller novels. The well-thumbed Secret Service training manuals told her just how seriously he took his job despite appearances.

They'd never found the sheets, but a single pillow had surfaced and a sleeping bag unzipped over them had been enough by the time exhaustion had taken them under.

Thankfully, the one thing he'd known exactly how to find had been condoms. There was a supply of them in Valentin's emergency med kit.

"If something happens where Valentin has to walk across broken glass and cuts his paws, they make a quick emergency bandage."

Based on his disorganization about everything else, it actually made her believe him.

"This is going to be awkward," Alex grimaced.

"Why?"

"Because I'm not supposed to fraternize with my protectees."

"Fraternize?"

"I'm not supposed to, uh, have any relationship with a protectee." He began dressing in sweatshirt and pants.

"We do not have a relationship. We had sex."

"Not supposed to do that either."

She waited until he was standing on one leg to slip on his sweatpants. Pushing off the counter, she ducked low and tackled him. He flew out the door. Valentin had slept along her side of the mattress. When the back of Alex's calves hit the dog, he'd tumbled backward onto the mattress.

Exactly where she wanted him.

## 16

"HEY, ALEX."

Alex froze five steps out his front door, and looked up at Bethany as she ran up the sidewalk. She was wearing Wonder Woman-red leggings and runners. Dripping sweat stained a deep-v of darkness on her black USSS t-shirt. Trixie panted hard at her side.

"About time you got your lazy ass up and moving. You know this isn't California where..." Her words trailed off and her eyes went wide as she looked over his shoulder.

He didn't need to turn as Valentin came up beside him and his front door clicked shut. It didn't close by itself.

"Nice dress," Bethany shot out, then grimaced an apology.

He glanced over his shoulder. What had looked amazing on last night's dance floor, and had spent most of the night on the kitchen floor where he'd stripped it off Tanya last night, looked severely out of place under the parking lot lights at six-thirty on a dark chilly morning. Even if it still looked incredible.

"Thanks," Tanya didn't sound at all put out. "I wish I had my running clothes; I would have gone with you."

Bethany opened her mouth, scowled at him, then closed it.

Tanya continued, "How hard was it not to say, 'Looks like you got your exercise already.'?"

Bethany smiled at her. "Pretty hard."

"Did I step in the middle of—"

"God no!" Bethany held up both her hands.

"I'm not her type," Alex decided that he could either join the conversation or be run over by it.

They both turned to look at him like he was a side of meat. Then Tanya simply raised her eyebrows in surprise at Bethany.

Bethany shrugged a reply.

Maybe it *was* safer to stay quiet.

Bethany headed for her place with Trixie at her side, but called back over her shoulder. "Don't let Baxter or Tibbets see you or you're a dead man."

Tanya was silent as he held the Jeep's door for her.

Valentin only groused a little about being put in the rear seat. "Your legs are shorter, buddy. You ride in back."

"She's very pretty."

"She is." Alex started the Jeep and looked in the headlight's spread to find a change of topic. All he found was an early robin listening for a worm under one of the manicured shrubs.

"She's not your type?"

"No. She said *I* wasn't..." Tanya had inverted the

sentence and it gave him pause. The beautiful blonde with the twangy West Virginia accent and a good sense of humor made him *feel* as if he should want her. But...

He looked over at Tanya watching him. "All these years I never knew what my type was. I guess now I do, Tanya."

For once, she didn't have anything snappy to say as he backed out of his spot and headed to her hotel.

Instead of stretching our for a nap on the back seat, Valentin rode with his big head between them so that Alex couldn't see Tanya's expression.

## 17

ALL WEEK, THERE WAS NO SIGN OF ANY ATTACK.

Instead, Tanya played her foreign policy game.

She took her meetings. Afterward, Alex offered interesting contexts from history she'd never studied, on just what they meant—really—and how to get around the blockades that were raised. Once the carefully routine afternoon changeovers were done, she shifted mode and let Carlton show her the sights of their capital. It should have been fun. He was intelligent, had grown up here, and clearly wanted her. There was a nice kind of charge when a man wanted you, but with each day she found less and less voltage in it.

With Alex, there was nothing but charge, a very high-energy one.

Each night he picked her up after Carlton's drop off.

Twice she and Alex had gone dancing.

But the nights they spent at his place with Valentin were the best.

The hotel was too neat, too perfect. She liked eating

Chinese food on the couch and making love on the low mattress—now that they'd opened enough boxes to find the sheets.

Each morning they ran together with Valentin, once with Bethany and both dogs. She was an easy woman to like, even though Valentin did his best to stay between them.

Ukrainian had about a two-thirds vocabulary overlap with Russian and Alex had a very sharp ear. Their lovemaking rapidly slid into Ukrainian; food soon followed.

If he still harbored Pushkinesque fantasies, he kept them to herself.

"I see two problems," she told him the morning of the fifth day as she lay in his arms. The mattress was still on the floor. Though about half of the boxes were unpacked, he still hadn't found the hardware for the frame.

"Give me a minute to recover before I try to solve one of them."

She kissed him briefly. He was very sweet.

"The second problem is that I'm supposed to fly home immediately after the treaty is signed in two days."

Alex just grunted unhappily. "The Secret Service isn't in the habit of posting its dog handlers to Kyiv."

"You'll miss the sex."

"Hell yeah."

Which was going to really irritate her for being his priority, even if she'd miss it too.

"At least half as much as I'll miss you," he growled out in a surly mashup of Ukrai-ssian which made her feel much better.

"Yes," she agreed carefully as she tested the thought inside. "Yes." In a single week she'd come to care about Alex Warren a great deal. Not once past the first meeting had he seen her as Pushkin's Tatyana Larina helplessly flailing against society's dictates and whims. Nor did he see her as Father did: a useful tool to fill an important government position, expanding his control. And definitely not as if she was a mere steppingstone toward advancement.

Alex saw her as his lover. As a crusader for Ukrainian rule for the Crimea. And as more of a person and less of a "woman" than she'd thought herself. Everyone always treated her as a woman first, until she'd believed that was most of what she was. But Alex, despite being her lover, seemed to bring her into focus—to herself—as a person.

Last night, after making love, they'd actually talked of her long-term plans for the future of reunifying Ukraine.

She'd never laid out the full scope of her plan to anyone, not even Father. It was an impossible task and the few she'd even partially revealed it to had laughed outright.

With Alex, they'd debated late into the night about just what it would take to achieve that goal based on the various countries' present-day geopolitical dynamics.

This morning they lay together in silence for a while, neither of them finding anything more to say about the fast-approaching end of their time together.

Finally Alex grumbled out, "What's the first problem?"

"The first problem—" Tanya took a deep breath. "You can not become strange with me about this."

Alex nodded his agreement.

"The first problem is...that I want to go to the Library of Congress this afternoon. They have a first edition of Pushkin's *Eugene Onegin.* I have had my embassy call and they've arranged for me to see it at the same time as your turnover to Carlton. Now, one unwise remark out of you and I'll... I'll... I will tell Valentin to sit on you."

He smiled. "Oh, I'm so afraid of my own dog."

Her typical "retributions" when Alex was being impossible about something could be very enjoyable as they typically ended in great sex. She'd never get enough of him and that "second problem" was a major one. But as to the first, if he did not behave...

"It would be my pleasure to escort you there, Ms. *Tatyana* Larina."

"Valentin!" She called to the dog where he slept close by her side of the bed. Tanya pointed at Alex's chest. "*Sidet'!*"

Valentin hopped to his feet, stepped lightly over her, and sat on Alex's chest.

"Goddamn it," Alex grunted as seventy-five kilos of dog landed squarely on him.

"*Myesto!*" She ordered him to Stay.

Then she slipped out of bed, and made a point of walking very slowly toward the shower while Alex tried to get his dog off his chest.

## 18

TANYA'S CRIMEAN CAMPAIGN, AS THEY NOW CALLED IT between themselves, had led him up and down embassy row and into both the Capitol Building, which was impressive, and the Pentagon, which was a little alarming. She was a true force of nature. Alex figured if anyone could actually achieve her so-unlikely objective, it would be Tanya Larina.

But Alex hadn't yet been to the Library of Congress.

He hated not being able to check out the premises before escorting Tanya there, but that had been the pattern of much of their week.

The Library of Congress lay east across the street from the Capitol Building, just south of the pillared Supreme Court Building. The broad marble steps zigzagged around either side of a large fountain.

"It is the court of the Neptune King," Tanya announced.

"King Neptune, the god of the sea. What is he doing guarding the Library of Congress?"

"I was thinking that might make sense to you Americans. It makes no sense to this Ukrainian."

Alex stared at the large bronze king. All about him, his courtiers blew fountains of water out the end of conch shells raised as trumpets. "It's because he visits here so often. You see, it's very hard to read books in his underwater kingdom. Of course, you wouldn't recognize him. He comes disguised as an out-of-practice scholar of old Russian literature."

Tanya turned to him and after a long moment whispered, "But I *do* recognize him, *Mishka.*"

Alex blinked. Little Bear. An endearment between girlfriend and boyfriend. Until this moment, they had avoided the little nicknames so common between Slavic couples. It felt both wonderful and painful, the former because of its truth and the latter because of its looming end. It was made even more appropriate by the big Russian bear dog presently leaning over the fountain for a drink of water.

But what was Tanya? *Tygrenya,* his "little tiger"? Or...

"*Drakonchyk.*"

Tanya blinked in surprise, then wrapped her arms around his neck and his Little Dragon kissed him most thoroughly.

"What?" He kept her close after the kiss.

"The way you see me...it is wonderful!"

A hard snarl from Valentin had him instantly shoving Tanya behind him and grabbing for his sidearm.

"What *I'm* seeing is going to knock you out of the goddamn service!" Carlton stepped right up into his face. "Fast!"

Ripper let out a hard snarl. He must have mistaken Carlton's snarled "Fast" for "*Fass*"—attack!

He leapt at Alex.

Before Alex could do more than raise an arm in self defense, Valentin casually raised a massive paw and swatted the Malinois aside, tumbling him into the fountain.

Ripper came out of the water in a fighting rage and leapt on Valentin. But even the Malinois' jaws were little match for Valentin's thick coat.

Valentin twisted far faster than anyone would expect from his bulk. He clamped his massive jaw down on the back of Ripper's Secret Service Kevlar vest, shook him free of his bite on Valentin's scruff, then tossed him back into the water as if he was a bath toy, not seventy pounds of furious attack dog.

Ripper braced to leap over the fountain's concrete edge. Alex could almost feel Valentin roll his eyes and sigh. Then he turned to face Ripper directly and braced himself for action. This was going to end badly for Ripper.

"You'd better call him off unless you want him hurt," Alex warned, keeping his body between Tanya and the near-apoplectic Carlton.

"*Fuss!*" Carlton snapped out. "*Platz!*"

Ripper's snarl still echoed deep in his chest as he climbed from the water and came to Heel. He gave himself a big shake that sprayed Carlton with near-freezing fountain water. But he didn't Lie Down.

Valentin tracked his every step very closely.

"*Ruhig!*" Alex ordered Ripper to be Quiet in German

while Carlton wiped at his own face. The Malinois obeyed, though his teeth remained bared.

Carlton looked even angrier that Alex could command his dog. It was a shortcoming that Valentin did not share. Except for his curious obedience to Tanya, Valentin would ignore anyone other than Alex himself.

"I have control now," Carlton snapped at him. "You are relieved of duty pending review. I will be reporting both of you to Captain Baxter."

Tanya stepped around him with what sounded like a truly foul Ukrainian imprecation but he thought might translate as "ducks are going to kick your ass." She'd told him that Ukrainians used Russian when they wanted a gutter-foul curse. Their native language leant itself mostly to insults.

"You," she jabbed a Ukrainian Fort 17 pistol under Carlton's chin, forcing him to tip his head back.

Alex had noticed the small 9mm in her purse several times but she was so smooth and practiced that he hadn't spotted her drawing it—a useful skill on a busy street. It was small enough that she almost appeared to have her fingers around Carlton's throat.

"You wish vengeance because his dog is stronger than yours," her voice was dangerously calm—stripped of all the lilt and emotion that normally made it so rich. "Or because he stops Russian attackers and you do not. Or he sleeps with me and you do not. Ah, I see that is what makes you angriest. I will tell you this, Lieutenant Carlton Tibbets, there was never a chance that I wanted to see if your tiny dick matched your massive ego." She used a sharp jab with her gun to send Carlton stumbling back.

Then the gun disappeared back into her purse, again with the smooth move of a professional. Alex kept forgetting that she'd been an elite soldier. A story that had come out after he'd had trouble waking her one time when she'd slept on her right ear.

"*I* make my choices," she was still browbeating Carlton. "Any man who interferes with them will answer to me first and your President tomorrow after he signs my treaty. "

Carlton's aristocratic affectations crumbled enough that he growled almost as dangerously as Ripper had.

Alex knew he had to break the tableau if he wanted any chance of keeping his job. And if he was fired from the Service...Valentin belonged to the US government, not to him. That *couldn't* be allowed to happen.

"Ms. Larina," he addressed her formally to try and get her out of soldier-mode. "You have an appointment with the Library of Congress librarian."

"Yes." She blew out a hard breath, then tugged down her jacket to shift it into place.

He'd have to tease her about acting like Captain Picard. Later.

"Yes. Let us go." She tugged the hem of her jacket again, making him smile. She spotted that and raised an eyebrow in question.

He made a show of tugging his own vest into place.

She glanced down at her hands. Then her smile said that *Star Trek* was something else they could enjoy together.

Without another word, she turned and headed up the stairs.

When he went to follow, Carlton ground out. "You're relieved, Warren."

"*Ko mne,*" Tanya called without turning.

Valentin had the decency to check in with him rather than just answering the Come command, literally To Me.

Alex offered a shrug to Carlton that said it was his decision.

Carlton was biting his tongue so hard that it had to hurt.

He finally waved a hand to proceed.

Alex signaled Valentin to run ahead and catch up with Tanya who'd kept climbing the stairs.

Ripper raced by Alex a moment later.

"Damn you to hell," Carlton said as they started up the steps together. He might have added, "Lucky bastard." But it was hard to tell.

## 19

Tanya was most of the way up the long flight of stairs when she noticed the change.

Ripper trotted ahead, close beside Valentin as if looking for an opening to attack the larger dog.

But between one step and the next, both dogs froze, but only for an instant.

Then, in unison, Valentin swung left and Ripper to the right. Then they swung back into line in front of her. All of their attention was at the head of the stairs.

"But there's no one there, boys."

The dogs ignored her.

They were on a scent.

Might it be the same scent they'd chased out behind the coffee shop on—

The next few moments happened so quickly, yet seemed to occur in such slow motion, that she could see every moment.

Just as her foot hit the top step, Ripper leapt at a shadow in the archway.

Halfway aloft, there was a sharp crack. It sounded like a gunshot...almost. But her training told her it was a Taser.

Ripper dropped like... Yes, he'd been Tasered! His body gone completely limp.

Valentin grabbed the shooter's arm in his jaw and whipped it sideways. There was another sharp crack, this time of his bone breaking. The man screamed until Valentin threw him into one of the marble columns that supported the entry arch. He hit headfirst and dropped to the ground beside Ripper.

That was the moment that Alex slammed into her from behind.

He took her down with a roll that had him taking the hit of slamming onto the stone entryway. He continued the roll until she was lying face down on the cold granite and he was spread-eagled over her.

There was a quick bark of gunfire.

Alex jerked atop her.

"Alex!" The scream ripped out of her. When she struggled to rise to see how badly he'd been hurt, he pushed her cheek down against the ground.

"Stay still."

Then, directly in her line of sight, a man in jeans and a light jacket dropped to the ground just a meter away. He had two large, red stains on his chest.

Blood. *He'd* been shot. Not Alex!

Alex shifted. Not off her, but as if reaching...

There was another crack of a firing Taser close by her good ear. He kept her pinned and she couldn't turn to see the third body that hit the ground, but she could certainly hear it.

## 20

ALEX CHECKED THE AREA AND THE ATTACKERS CAREFULLY before shifting off Tanya.

When she tried to stand, he pushed her back down to sit on the top step. "I had to take you down pretty hard. Just give yourself a moment."

She nodded vaguely. He could see the adrenaline letdown shakes kick in, but she didn't appear to be injured.

Perp Number Three was still out with a pair of Taser leads that Alex had fired into his chest.

Perp Number Two was dead on the ground with Carlton's two bullets in his chest.

Perp Number One was groaning awake after Valentin's abuse.

Alex handcuffed him, even with the shattered arm, then patted him down. The man wore flesh-toned gloves. When he forced open the man's good hand, he spotted a small spray bottle, and froze.

Novichok was all he could think. The Russians had

tried to kill Sergei Skripal, a former spy, in the UK. They'd almost taken out him and his daughter. The poison had also nearly killed several of the investigators.

Very carefully, he bagged the toxic nerve agent.

Valentin stood poised to attack the man again as he groaned, coming to full consciousness.

"*Domoy!*" he ordered.

Valentin didn't need him to point to know that he should Go Home to Tanya. It was only as Tanya was reaching out to embrace him that the risk sunk in. If any of the poison was on Valentin's fur—

"Sit, Valentin. *Sidet'!*" Valentin froze halfway between them and sat.

Tanya reached out.

"No! Don't touch him!" She too froze, then looked at him in surprise.

Alex checked to see what Carlton was doing. But he hadn't moved. His FN P90 submachine gun was still clenched in his hands...with the safety off.

Alex crossed to him, clicked the safety on, and then pushed the gun down until it rested once more against Carlton's chest.

"I—" Carlton blinked hard but looked like he was only halfway back. "I've never had to actually shoot someone before."

"I know. It's hard. But you did the right thing." Then he remembered what a long-ago partner had done for him. So, he just stopped to chat—in a normal tone—for a moment as if everything was fine and they hadn't all three just almost died. "You get through it."

Carlton blinked at him.

"I was in counterfeiting before I hit the Uniformed Division. One operation went down ugly. I had to take out two men and a woman. You'll get the shakes later. Don't worry. It's normal."

"And you decided UD would be less dangerous?" Carlton was most of the way back. Took his hands off his weapon.

"The Service decided that if I could do that, I belonged in Protection. That was a headache I didn't want, so I managed to get on a dog team. And once I met Valentin…" he shrugged.

Carlton nodded again, then spun around and spotted Ripper struggling to his feet. Carlton knelt and dragged his dog against his chest.

Alex knelt with him. Carlton's eyes were now focused…and surprisingly close to tears as he embraced Ripper.

Carlton scanned around. He had to clear his throat again before he could speak, "So, what've we got?"

Alex just held up the small spray bottle in the clear plastic bag.

To his credit, it didn't take him but a second before he froze exactly as Alex had.

"Yeah, I know. It's your detail. Call it in."

While Carlton was calling in a full team: agents, security, an ambulance, and a full hazmat team, Alex doublechecked Ripper.

The dog had survived the human-sized jolt of electricity, but appeared otherwise unhurt. He'd wager the poor animal had a hell of a headache. At least he'd never touched the poisoner.

Alex looked again at Valentin who appeared very frustrated at not being allowed to go to Tanya. There still could be poison on his fur.

"Carlton, tell them to bring dog-grooming clippers, too. Big ones."

## 21

THE RARE BOOK ROOM AT THE LIBRARY OF CONGRESS wasn't what she'd expected.

Tanya had assumed it was the central room that sat beneath the great copper dome of the Thomas Jefferson Building with its circular reading desks arranged like a giant bullseye around the librarian's central desk, multi-story mezzanines, and giant statuary of the Muses. It was always the room they showed in movies and it seemed very special.

Instead, Alex led her through that room and up a flight of stairs.

Even after two days he still had a slight limp from a knee he'd twisted while taking the brunt of their fall.

She shivered again at how close it had been.

Novichok nerve agent. A single spray to her face and she'd be dead by now. That tiny bottle would be enough to kill hundreds.

Though Russia had denied any involvement, the three men's scorpion tattoos marked them as 25th Special

Forces Brigade Spetsnaz. The surviving soldiers would probably never crack, but the CIA had whisked them away and she didn't envy their future.

President Zachary Thomas had invited the Russian ambassador to the signing of her treaty—despite it being between the US, Turkey, and Ukraine.

And she'd been just close enough to hear the President whisper to him, "Don't even *think* about asking for prisoner return or we might see how you like being sprayed with that shit. Tell your FSB that Moscow itself will deeply regret it the next time they bring a nerve agent into my country or attempt a murder on my soil." He had paused for a long moment, then continued. "We will consider it a declaration of war."

It had taken her by surprise, until she understood that the President knew exactly who and who couldn't overhear his threat. So had the Russian ambassador who had blanched white. He might hate her more now, but it was with good reason. The move had poisoned the Russian-American relationship even further as assuredly as if the Novichok had indeed been sprayed.

Through the main part of the Library of Congress, Alex led her up the head of the stairs and stepped through simple wooden double doors. On the other side was a vast space. Not brilliantly lit by sunlight like the Main Reading Room. Instead, the wide space was dim, without being dark. A crystal chandelier hanging from the high ceiling seemed to be the only adornment to the white walls framed by thick trimwork and accented by dark red carpet. The reading tables were simple wooden affairs and the chairs no fancier.

It was as if the designer had said, "In the Rare Book Room, it is the only the books that matter."

Some books were on display, but most, she knew were kept in vaults below.

They were guided to a table where a small book nestled in a v-shaped plexiglass form. It was open to the page Alex had requested. A librarian wearing white gloves stood nearby to turn to any other pages they requested.

"How rare is this thing?" Alex whispered.

The librarian cleared her throat gently. "Just last year, a copy in similar condition sold for five hundred and eighty-thousand dollars."

Tanya tucked her hands into her back pockets to make sure she resisted any urge to reach out and touch it.

"Valentin," Alex addressed his dog sitting next to them. "Stop shedding." It was a funny joke, just barely.

"Poor Valentin," Tanya whispered. This room was definitely a place of whispers.

His dog had been fully shaved right there on the Library of Congress steps by two men in full bio-hazard suits. Subsequent tests showed that some of his fur had indeed been exposed to the Novichok. Probably not a lethal dose if she'd touched him, but she might have become very, very sick. His thick fur had protected him. Not anymore. Until he regrew his heavy double-layer coat, he only looked large instead of bear huge.

It had been while Alex was squatting in front of Valentin and telling him what a good boy he was while being clipped, that she'd asked the question.

"How did they know I'd be at here at this exact time?"

Both Alex and Carlton had turned slowly to look at her, then at each other. Finally, all three of them had turned to look west to where the Ukrainian embassy stood. Tanya had followed her own agenda except on two occasions. Her original departure from the embassy, and her trip to the library of Congress.

Ambassador Tomas Khomenko had indeed been a leftover from the Soviet era. In fact, it seemed that he'd been working with the new Russian Federation for most of his career. Perhaps even had a role in the success of the annexation of Crimea. After she'd alerted her father and they'd sent internal security to take him, Tomas Khomenko had shot himself.

Just this morning, the Ukrainian President had called her—thankfully not a video chat as she'd still been in Alex's bed when she took the call. He partly wanted to congratulate her on the signing of the treaty, but also to offer her the position of Ambassador to the United States.

There hadn't even been a moment to doubt. From Washington, DC, she'd have exceptional access to all of the political connections she would need, both foreign and American.

And there was another reason.

The moment she'd hung up the call, she'd thrown herself at Alex. She'd have to figure out how to tell Father and the President about him later.

"Getting shaved. Hell of a birthday present," Alex was still talking to Valentin much to the amusement of the patiently waiting rare-book librarian.

"Birthday?"

"Today is Saint Valentine's Day. That's his birthday.

He's having steak tonight but no candles—he eats those. Crayons too. He has this thing for wax."

"I'll make sure to remember that."

At Alex's happy smile that there'd be a reason for her to remember it in the future, Tanya slipped her hand into his.

"Saint Valen*teen's* Day," she whispered after kissing him lightly. "Do you think he will mind sharing his day with us, *Mishka?*"

Alex tightened his clasp on her hand and rested his other on Valentin's head.

"I don't think your Little Bear or *our* Russian bear dog will mind at all, Ms. Tatyana Larina."

She couldn't find it in herself to put much heat into the scowl she aimed his way.

"*Ko mne, Drakonchyk.*" Come, my Little Dragon.

The three of them leaned forward and Alex read the exposed passage aloud:

> *And so Tatyana was her name,*
> *Nor by her sister's brilliancy*
> *Nor by her beauty she became*
> *The attraction of every eye.*

# OFF THE LEASH (EXCERPT)

IF YOU ENJOYED THAT, YOU'LL LOVE THE NOVELS!

# OFF THE LEASH (EXCERPT)

"You're joking."

"Nope. That's his name. And he's yours now."

Sergeant Linda Hamlin wondered quite what it would take to wipe that smile off Lieutenant Jurgen's face. A 120mm round from an M1A1 Abrams Main Battle Tank came to mind.

The kennel master of the US Secret Service's Canine Team was clearly a misogynistic jerk from the top of his polished head to the bottoms of his equally polished boots. She wondered if the shoelaces were polished as well.

Then she looked over at the poor dog sitting hopefully on the concrete kennel floor. His stall had a dog bed three times his size and a water bowl deep enough for him to bathe in. No toys, because toys always came from the handler as a reward. He offered her a sad sigh and a liquid doggy gaze. The kennel even smelled wrong, more of sanitizer than dog. The walls seemed to echo with each bark down the long line of kennels housing the candidate hopefuls for the next addition to the Secret Service's team.

Thor—really?—was a brindle-colored mutt, part who-knew and part no-one-cared. He looked like a cross between an oversized, long-haired schnauzer and a dust mop that someone had spilled dark gray paint on. After mixing in streaks of tawny brown, they'd left one white paw just to make him all the more laughable.

And of course Lieutenant Jerk Jurgen would assign Thor to the first woman on the USSS K-9 team.

Unable to resist, she leaned over far enough to scruff the dog's ears. He was the physical opposite of the sleek and powerful Malinois MWDs—military war dogs—that she'd been handling for the 75th Rangers for the last five years. They twitched with eagerness and nerves. A good MWD was seventy pounds of pure drive—every damn second of the day. If the mild-mannered Thor weighed thirty pounds, she'd be surprised. And he looked like a little girl's best friend who should have a pink bow on his collar.

Jurgen was clearly ex-Marine and would have no respect for the Army. Of course, having been in the Army's Special Operations Forces, she knew better than to respect a Marine.

"We won't let any old swabbie bother us, will we?"

Jurgen snarled—definitely Marine Corps. Swabbie was slang for a Navy sailor and a Marine always took offense at being lumped in with them no matter how much they belonged. Of course the swabbies took offense at having the Marines lumped with *them*. Too bad there weren't any Navy around so that she could get two for the price of one. Jurgen wouldn't be her boss, so appeasing him wasn't high on her to-do list.

At least she wouldn't need any of the protective bite gear working with Thor. With his stature, he was an explosives detection dog without also being an attack one.

"Where was he trained?" She stood back up to face the beast.

"Private outfit in Montana—some place called Henderson's Ranch. Didn't make their MWD program," his scoff said exactly what he thought the likelihood of any dog outfit in Montana being worthwhile. "They wanted us to try the little runt out."

She'd never heard of a training program in Montana. MWDs all came out of Lackland Air Force Base training. The Secret Service mostly trained their own and they all came from Vohne Liche Kennels in Indiana. Unless... Special Operations Forces dogs were trained by private contractors. She'd worked beside a Delta Force dog for a single month—he'd been incredible.

"Is he trained in English or German?" Most American MWDs were trained in German so that there was no confusion in case a command word happened to be part of a spoken sentence. It also made it harder for any random person on the battlefield to shout something that would confuse the dog.

"German according to his paperwork, but he won't listen to me much in either language."

Might as well give the diminutive Thor a few basic tests. A snap of her fingers and a slap on her thigh had the dog dropping into a smart "heel" position. No need to call out *Fuss—by my foot.*

"*Pass auf!*" Guard! She made a pistol with her thumb and forefinger and aimed it at Jurgen as she grabbed her forearm with her other hand—the military hand sign for enemy.

The little dog snarled at Jurgen sharply enough to have him backing out of the kennel. "Goddamn it!"

"*Ruhig.*" Quiet. Thor maintained his fierce posture but dropped the snarl.

"*Gute Hund.*" Good dog, Linda countered the command.

Thor looked up at her and wagged his tail happily. She tossed him a doggie treat, which he caught midair and crunched happily.

She didn't bother looking up at Jurgen as she knelt once more to check over the little dog. His scruffy fur was so soft that it tickled. Good strength in the jaw, enough to show he'd had bite training despite his size—perfect if she ever needed to take down a three-foot-tall terrorist. Legs said he was a jumper.

"Take your time, Hamlin. I've got nothing else to do with the rest of my goddamn day except babysit you and this mutt."

"Is the course set?"

"Sure. Take him out," Jurgen's snarl sounded almost as nasty as Thor's before he stalked off.

She stood and slapped a hand on her opposite shoulder.

Thor sprang aloft as if he was attached to springs and she caught him easily. He'd cleared well over double his own height. Definitely trained...and far easier to catch than seventy pounds of hyperactive Malinois.

She plopped him back down on the ground. On lead or off? She'd give him the benefit of the doubt and try off first to see what happened.

Linda zipped up her brand-new USSS jacket against the cold and led the way out of the kennel into the hard sunlight of the January morning. Snow had brushed the higher hills around the USSS James J. Rowley Training Center—which this close to Washington, DC, wasn't saying much—but was melting quickly. Scents wouldn't carry as well on the cool air, making it more of a challenge for Thor to locate the explosives. She didn't know where they were either. The course was a test for handler as well as dog.

Jurgen would be up in the observer turret looking for any excuse to mark down his newest team. Perhaps teasing him about being just a Marine hadn't been her best tactical choice. She sighed. At least she was consistent—she'd always been good at finding ways to piss people off before she could stop herself and consider the wisdom of doing so.

This test was the culmination of a crazy three months, so she'd forgive herself this time—something she also wasn't very good at.

In October she'd been out of the Army and unsure what to do next. Tucked in the packet with her DD 214 honorable discharge form had been a flyer on career opportunities with the US Secret Service dog team: *Be all your dog can be!* No one else being released from Fort

Benning that day had received any kind of a job flyer at all that she'd seen, so she kept quiet about it.

She had to pass through DC on her way back to Vermont—her parent's place. Burlington would work for, honestly, not very long at all, but she lacked anywhere else to go after a decade of service. So, she'd stopped off in DC to see what was up with that job flyer. Five interviews and three months to complete a standard six-month training course later—which was mostly a cakewalk after fighting with the US Rangers—she was on-board and this chill January day was her first chance with a dog. First chance to prove that she still had it. First chance to prove that she hadn't made a mistake in deciding that she'd seen enough bloodshed and war zones for one lifetime and leaving the Army.

The Start Here sign made it obvious where to begin, but she didn't dare hesitate to take in her surroundings past a quick glimpse. Jurgen's score would count a great deal toward where she and Thor were assigned in the future. Mostly likely on some field prep team, clearing the way for presidential visits.

As usual, hindsight informed her that harassing the lieutenant hadn't been an optimal strategy. A hindsight that had served her equally poorly with regular Army commanders before she'd finally hooked up with the Rangers—kowtowing to officers had never been one of her strengths.

Thankfully, the Special Operations Forces hadn't given a damn about anything except performance and *that* she could always deliver, since the day she'd been named the team captain for both soccer and volleyball.

She was never popular, but both teams had made all-state her last two years in school.

The canine training course at James J. Rowley was a two-acre lot. A hard-packed path of tramped-down dirt led through the brown grass. It followed a predictable pattern from the gate to a junker car, over to tool shed, then a truck, and so on into a compressed version of an intersection in a small town. Beyond it ran an urban street of gray clapboard two- and three-story buildings and an eight-story office tower, all without windows. Clearly a playground for Secret Service training teams.

Her target was the town, so she blocked the city street out of her mind. Focus on the problem: two roads, twenty storefronts, six houses, vehicles, pedestrians.

It might look normal...normalish with its missing windows and no movement. It would be anything but. Stocked with fake IEDs, a bombmaker's stash, suicide cars, weapons caches, and dozens of other traps, all waiting for her and Thor to find. He had to be sensitive to hundreds of scents and it was her job to guide him so that he didn't miss the opportunity to find and evaluate each one.

There would be easy scents, from fertilizer and diesel fuel used so destructively in the 1995 Oklahoma City bombing, to almost as obvious TNT to the very difficult to detect C-4 plastic explosive.

Mannequins on the street carried grocery bags and briefcases. Some held fresh meat, a powerful smell demanding any dog's attention, but would count as a false lead if they went for it. On the job, an explosives detection dog wasn't supposed to care about anything except explosives. Other mannequins were wrapped in suicide vests loaded with Semtex or wearing knapsacks filled with package bombs made from Russian PVV-5A.

She spotted Jurgen stepping into a glassed-in observer turret atop the corner drugstore. Someone else was already there and watching.

She looked down once more at the ridiculous little dog and could only hope for the best.

"Thor?"

He looked up at her.

She pointed to the left, away from the beaten path.

"*Such!*" Find.

Thor sniffed left, then right. Then he headed forward quickly in the direction she pointed.

———

CLIVE ANDREWS SAT IN THE SECOND-STORY WINDOW AT THE corner of Main and First, the only two streets in town. Downstairs was a drugstore all rigged to explode, except there were no triggers and there was barely enough explosive to blow up a candy box.

Not that he'd know, but that's what Lieutenant Jurgen had promised him.

It didn't really matter if it was rigged to blow for real, because when Miss Watson—never Ms. or Mrs.—asked for a "favor," you did it. At least he did. Actually, he had yet to meet anyone else who knew her. Not that he'd asked around. She wasn't the sort of person one talked about with strangers, or even close friends. He'd bet even if they did, it would be in whispers. That's just what she was like.

So he'd traveled across town from the White House and into Maryland on a cold winter's morning, barely past a sunrise that did nothing to warm the day. Now he sat in an unheated glass icebox and watched a new officer run a test course he didn't begin to understand. Lieutenant Jurgen settled in beside him at a console with feeds from a dozen cameras and banks of switches.

While waiting, Clive had been fooling around with a sketch on a small pad of paper. The next State Dinner was in seven days. President Zachary Taylor had invited the leaders of Vietnam, Japan, and the Philippines to the White House for discussions about some Chinese islands. Or something like that, Clive hadn't really been paying attention to the details past the attendee list.

Instead, he was contemplating the dessert for such a dinner that would surprise, perhaps delight, as well as being an icebreaker for future discussions. Being the chocolatier for the White House was the most exciting job he'd ever had. Every challenge was fresh and new, like the first strawberry of each year.

This one would be elegant. January was a little early, it would be better if it was spring, but that wasn't crucial. A large half-egg shape of paper-thin white chocolate filled with a mousse—white chocolate? No, nor a dark chocolate. Instead, a milk chocolate mousse but rich with flavor, perhaps bourbon. Then mold the dark chocolate to top it with a filigree bird, wings spread in half flight, ready to soar upward. A crane perhaps? He made a note to check with the protocol office to make sure that he wouldn't be offending some leader without knowing it.

"Never underestimate the power of a good dessert," he mumbled one of Jacques Torres' favorite admonitions. This was going to work very nicely.

"What's that?" Jurgen grunted out without looking up.

"Just talking to myself."

Which earned him a dismissive grunt, as if he was unworthy of the agent's attention. It wouldn't surprise him.

———

*Keep reading now!*
*Available at fine retailers everywhere.*
*Off the Leash*

## ABOUT THE AUTHOR

USA Today and Amazon #1 Bestseller M. L. "Matt" Buchman started writing on a flight from Japan to ride his bicycle across the Australian Outback. Just part of a solo around-the-world trip that ultimately launched his writing career.

From the very beginning, his powerful female heroines insisted on putting character first, *then* a great adventure. He's since written over 70 action-adventure thrillers and military romantic suspense novels. And just for the fun of it: 100 short stories, and a fast-growing pile of read-by-author audiobooks.

Booklist says: "3X Top 10 of the Year." PW says: "Tom Clancy fans open to a strong female lead will clamor for more." His fans say: "I want more now...of everything." That his characters are even more insistent than his fans is a hoot.

As a 30-year project manager with a geophysics degree who has designed and built houses, flown and jumped out of planes, and solo-sailed a 50' ketch, he is awed by what is possible. More at: www.mlbuchman.com.

# Other works by M. L. Buchman: *(\* - also in audio)*

## Other works by M. L. Buchman:

### Contemporary Romance (cont)

**Love Abroad**
*Heart of the Cotswolds: England*
*Path of Love: Cinque Terre, Italy*

**Where Dreams**
*Where Dreams are Born*
*Where Dreams Reside*
*Where Dreams Are of Christmas\**
*Where Dreams Unfold*
*Where Dreams Are Written*

### Science Fiction / Fantasy

**Deities Anonymous**
*Cookbook from Hell: Reheated*
*Saviors 101*

**Single Titles**
*The Nara Reaction*
*Monk's Maze*
*the Me and Elsie Chronicles*

### Non-Fiction

**Strategies for Success**
*Managing Your Inner Artist/Writer*
*Estate Planning for Authors\**
*Character Voice*
*Narrate and Record Your Own*
*Audiobook\**

## Short Story Series by M. L. Buchman:

### Romantic Suspense

**Delta Force**
*Th Delta Force Shooters*
*The Delta Force Warriors*

**Firehawks**
*The Firehawks Lookouts*
*The Firehawks Hotshots*
*The Firebirds*

**The Night Stalkers**
*The Night Stalkers 5D Stories*
*The Night Stalkers 5E Stories*
*The Night Stalkers CSAR*
*The Night Stalkers Wedding Stories*

**US Coast Guard**

**White House Protection Force**

### Contemporary Romance

**Eagle Cove**

**Henderson's Ranch\***

**Where Dreams**

### Action-Adventure Thrillers

**Dead Chef**

**Miranda Chase Origin Stories**

### Science Fiction / Fantasy

**Deities Anonymous**

**Other**
*The Future Night Stalkers*
*Single Titles*

# SIGN UP FOR M. L. BUCHMAN'S NEWSLETTER TODAY

*and receive:*
*Release News*
*Free Short Stories*
*a Free Book*

*Get your free book today. Do it now.*
*free-book.mlbuchman.com*

www.ingramcontent.com/pod-product-compliance
Lightning Source LLC
Chambersburg PA
CBHW060631130626
46555CB00002B/755